THE YACK YACK

The Yack Yack

New York Notes and Stories

by

JUDYTH EMANUEL

Adelaide Books
New York / Lisbon
2022

The Yack Yack

New York Notes and Stories

By Judyth Emanuel

Published by Adelaide Books, New York / Lisbon
adelaidebooks.org

Editor-in-Chief
Stevan V. Nikolic

For any information, please address Adelaide Books
at info@adelaidebooks.org

or write to:

Adelaide Books
244 Fifth Ave. Suite D27
New York, NY, 10001

ISBN: 978-1-955196-79-6

Printed in the United States of America

For Miss K and Moo

Katherine Rose and Maximilian

some yacketty yack

Contents

the bloom and the seedy and holy and black jeeps and beauty
salons and scaffolding and ma'am how do you like your eggs

you have to pull everything apart to make any sense

notes

the near miss

I am the near miss woman owning a different reality, cursing high shelves, wandering into my own particular story, never forgetting it's a lie that God created the world but believing something must have created the world, because the world is so intricate and beautiful. I am a woman who does not have the time to chant but then not many people do. I understand everything has its limits, ambivalence often overtakes me yet I crave the depth of a volcano, being a romanticist from the antipodes, which sounds so fine, which is Australia, an island obsessing about basketball, football, cricket, all games played with a ridiculous ball. I really think sport sucks and I have fallen in love with New York City, which I will bang on about with more and more endless amorous descriptions, being dreams pushing aside sense and structure and superego and truth and joining the dots that are really a city that is fast and incredible of noise, sugar, the absence of prayers and a great passion for the arts sounding and looking and engaging with opera being one of the arts, like The Barber of Seville cursed at first with a disastrous opening night in 1816 when the music teacher tripped over and got a nose bleed and a cat wandered on stage. Still beauty and lechery always prove a great success. In 1916 at The Metropolitan Opera House, I am sitting in Row F for fabulous watching The Barber of Seville, this feast of frivolity, setting the mind aflame and the very touching thing of even a real horse and a real Labrador on stage for the finale.

lost in the city

There was a time, a couple of years previously, before I met my friend, that I found myself lost in New York and I wonder how does that make any sense? A woman finding herself lost? But I did find myself, I did get lost pretty much every day and it was only for two weeks that I didn't have a single conversation and I felt my entire persona radiated a loud aura of nerdy and multitudinous klutziness and basic worry with the addition of fear that nobody knew where I was and did anyone care? So I went to Kinkos on Sixth Avenue every other day and paid fifteen dollars to email friends because I had no clue as to how to connect my laptop to the Internet in the place I was renting.

Yet at that time, I really did come to New York to be alone. To distance myself from the harsh fact of being a divorced single mother for the second time. Also, I thought it might be nice to find a lover, to be alone but to have a lover, but of course that never happened. I mean I looked good, being as thin as I was ever going to be, but I never spoke a word to anyone, not even to the man who followed me around the Whitney or the man who smiled at me buying lemon drizzle cake in the bakery section of Dean & Deluca or the movie star staring at me in MoMA, who I should have been staring at because he was famous, but instead he was staring at me, which happened sometimes when I was wearing a vague expression on my face, the dreaming face of someone deep in thought, anyway, I quickly looked away.

Wisdom told me, learn from your mistakes and I made so many mistakes and I never learned. But I possessed the expertise in making terrible choices with recipes involving meat dishes and booking random flights to leave the country and flying off to anywhere that was overcrowded and would accept me, so give me a medal for that and for having the inability to joyously romp and plunge into the splendid light of restless freedom.

As a timid traveler, I will never be a successful seagull, those white-winged birds crossing the sea in a wave of hideous squawking. I fly Qantas and sit obediently in my allocated seat with the seat belt buckled and swallow two Temazepam pills and drink as much alcohol as the airline allows me to.

These thoughts on leaving the country of my birth, my family that is now much diminished, my friends also mostly melted away. Farewell to the vast expanses, to the need to keep in touch. Goodbye to the young and the marrieds, who strive to become the stars of their own lives, this new phenomenon that I find both intriguing and revolting, the sort of people that clutter their houses with selfies and cover the door of the refrigerator with pictures of their hideous babies.

Hello to the exhilaration of a city floating on a vast watery floor, a most extravagant city owning a story of the rushing bigness and bravery and insolence, this proud panting behemoth.

Second warning, be prepared for countless descriptions of indescribable, high wattage clamor, defiance and congratulate me for possessing the skill of babbling.

That time alone in New York, the pure anonymity, being a speck, specking about the city late in March, on the edge of a brooding spring, avoiding the great wilderness, where the tall grow taller, realizing most of the residents of New York have escaped their origins of somewhere mind-numbingly boring, a place constricted by religion, where strip malls line the freeways and these misfits come to town to seek fulfillment, fame and getting lonely in a city of perpetual change, for the human element cannot compete with the stone and glass and the over achievement of self-renewal.

These are the times without maps, the days of getting lost, wandering on the peripheral, always the outsider, sounds more lyrical than the real circumstances of my stumbling through the galleries in the Meatpacking district feeling like an intruder or sitting with a million tourists on the steps of The Metropolitan Museum of Art thinking about art, what I am supposed to think about art, how much I love looking at art, how all I can do is look at the paintings and ask myself, am I truly engaged with the work? How thick I was at the time, thinking about the absence of lightning, the absence of love in my life, about being invisible, overcome with sweet meditations, hesitating at the top of the subway steps and wondering what subterranean hell awaited down below at 96th Street Station so I walked a thousand blocks just to be with myself, not because I was scared.

I stayed in a loft on 18th Street. In the early evenings, I stood in front of the loft's huge window, the prisoner of myself, watching a young couple in the apartment across the street. This happiness, laughter, as they arranged flowers, poured flutes of champagne and greeted guests for dinner, a get-together amassing conviviality, the entitlement of being a couple being a shield against restlessness, of being cocooned, a protection from loneliness, far removed from a single female lurker, pathetic at lurking, of retaining a melancholic disposition, another way of saying, I stank at socializing and I was the opposite of audacious, but if there was an emergency or a war, I knew without doubt, I would be heroic, but for now I put on my pajamas and bed socks and began flicking through a thousand television channels of another night in New York, capital of the world.

Here this perfect solitude to gather the hoots and the hollers, eavesdrop on sentiments, boastings, the spent hours searching for cake until I was lightheaded, the geek of me awakened, telling myself I felt at home here, pushing myself through the door of some café, the whole place frantic with lunchtime rush hour, a few surreptitious writers scribbling on scraps of paper in corner booths, loads of office-type girls drinking dreadful coffee and sighing into laptops, the dirty tables, the weak smoothies, an interior of a privileged life in a city hanging itself from subway straps and thanking god this city refused to sort the sane from the mad. I asked the waiter for another refill. Never take three cups of coffee for granted, whoa, I was so ecstatic and awake.

Here the curious glances of the baffled, the drifters, the failed wore ten layers of clothes and crouched in the doorways of derelict buildings remembering their history of love, the hints of love, being loved by a beloved in this city of passion, of hope, where the pleasurable emerged from the mists on the foggiest days, the winter drizzle reinforcing a thirst for a spectacle, for epic surfaces, for chaos. Let me be part of the herd, the chase, the move move move, the slippery, the ice-masses, not tempted by the tree of knowledge, but feed me doughnuts, allow the absolute metropolis to slide into my consciousness. For I was the unsteady interloper discovering that black ice was a threat to balance and dignity.

I was the displaced inside the city's belly with its giant's breath and me the crumb in its steaminess, its sweatiness, the roar, ignore the roar, the roar in my notes, a lost roar, the mouse of a roar.

the apartment

Now the happier times, for one month each year my friend and I swap the heat of summer in Australia for the sparseness of a New York winter by exchanging my house in Sydney for Chris and Helga's apartment in New York City.

On the first home exchange, my friend worries about the apartment.

What if it's a terrible place? Have you seen any pictures of the apartment?

Well sort of. Don't worry. It's New York. I don't care if we stay in a closet.

I do. I'm too big to fit inside a closet.

On a cold January day, we arrive at 415 Central Park West. The gist of it, the details, the story of a comfortable life, this art deco lobby, its honeyed lights and leadlight windows. The doorman hails us as if we are family. He loads our bags onto a shiny brass trolley. We follow him deeper into the shiny, more than shiny brass elevator rising to the top floor, top of the world unlocking the front door and walking into a place to shine in, with a momentous hugging spectacular view of Central Park and the city skyline. Here inside the apartment, gilt framed paintings line a hallway the color of butter and a whopping sleigh bed shall be the imperious king of the bedroom. The kitchen of my dreams, with a hand beaten copper sink, a monster coffee machine almost human, but far too clean to be human, this appliance boasts levers and switches, all the bells and whistles and I am terrified of it. The centerpiece of the kitchen is a French cream enameled stove with plenty of knobs and the sitting room has a fireplace with an the ornate mantel and there taking up an entire wall, a television that is monstrous in a good way.

Wow, I say to my friend, It's longer than the length of you. But not as wide.

The seventeenth floor, don't look out the windows, the fear of heights kicks in, fright looks down, fright feels dizzy, it's impossible to stand near the windows. My imagination in overdrive, I picture evil gravity sucking me out the window, begging me to jump, this jump-start belief that in a former life,

I fell from a great height. The remedy, I decide, is to pretend the apartment is on the ground floor. Imagine the view is enlarged postcards stuck to the windows. I lecture myself on how to be brave, how to acclimatize to a new place. Eat cookies. My friend says I'm nuts. He loves nuts. Every night after dinner, he fills a small bowl with almonds or cashews and he crunches and crunches. Not everyone loves nuts.

This apartment understands the need for objects as a reflection of oneself. These objects lovingly collected, construct a chronology of past lives revealing secret stories and a history of collecting bric-a-brac, like stuffed and plastic animals, a Polaroid land camera Model 95A, a Lindstrom's Gold Star pinball machine and two crossed teaspoons glued onto a china plate from the New York World's Fair 1789-1939. A tapestry of Trenton Princeton First Troop 1774. A weathered rocking horse leans against the kitchen wall, below a wooden roulette wheel the exact size of a bicycle wheel and tucked in the wire spokes of the roulette wheel is a handmade card with a drawing of a huge red heart, under which a son in the guise of his own son, has written, *Grandma Happy Valentine's Day. Thank you for giving my Mommy and Daddy a break! Love Declan.*

These impractical objects make me feel at home. An unopened can of Pork Slap Pale Ale on the bookshelf beside a paperbark moose about twelve inches high. The carefully molded papier-mâché goat's head in the second bathroom. On the window ledge, a big pink pig stands on the points of its hooves. A cork protrudes from the pig's belly. I take a closer look. A piggy bank, empty of coins but weighty, as heavy as the worn wooden bowling balls on the mantel. On a wooden church pew, I find a Moto Lita steering wheel, look no hands, a teaspoon collection of spoons in the shape of delicate shells all pastel colors, two fencing swords, a rusting fencing mask and twin Gatsby wooden tennis rackets. An antique cello case, this proud musical character leaning in the alcove near the front door. A yellow tin toy called The Jitterbug One Man Band dances on top of an open Louis Vuitton leather trunk beside the bed. A yellowing book, its loving title, Joseph Breck & Sons Illustrated Agricultural Hardware Implements Catalogue listing sheep shears, bouquet clippers and grass hooks. These implements, necessary and enticing. And on the bookshelves a small brown ceramic piglet beside three cast iron pigs one on top of each other, also a forlorn rabbit imprisoned inside a snow dome and a bunny covered in silver sequins dressed for a party.

In the corner of the apartment's living room sits a plush toy dog about thirty-five inches of extreme realism. This dog, not a real dog, stares blindly through vintage Chapal driving goggles, giving it a sinister appearance. The dog makes me uncomfortable. The dog glares unceasingly at me. I try to act nonchalant and creep over to the dog, not a real dog. I turn the dog around to face the window. That's better. Now the dog can observe the city from a distance, which should give him something to think about and keep him entertained.

The television monster bombards us with relentless advertisements. Stool softeners, fungal infections, vaginal douches, Brawny paper towels and Digger the Dermatophyte hides under deformed toenails. A million medications for heart, liver, erectile dysfunction and cholesterol followed by announcements spewing frightening side-effects like who cares if your heart fails, you pee involuntarily or your hair falls out strand by strand.

My friend obsessively unpacks and repacks his suitcase. Which drives me crazy.

Are you going to do this for the whole four weeks? Why can't you hang your clothes in the wardrobe like a normal person?

Winter in the city, sometimes the trudge of a storm and the value of a thick scarf and woolly ear muffs and fur trimmed leather gloves keep my fingers from turning blue and a black beret I love to wear and here I become just a salmon swimming up a waterfall city letting it gush all over me.

My friend and I are the embodiment of bickering shambolic travelers, the way-out out-of-towners, innocents abroad with a weakness for hash browns, an ability to tolerate brewed coffee, a deep hatred for the all-you-can-eat and without plans, except to find universal magnificence and interesting coats and bars with open fires. So with misguided determination, we make our way through the snow and slush to explore the precious and lively boroughs, all the time I am thinking about what we are not, nor will we ever be, that special breed, native New Yorkers. For opportunities and ideas come too late in life.

On we walked and on we walked and on we walked.

the yack yack the painted stares

The Upper West Side, the yack-yack neighborhood, grows literary old peckers, fruits, the mutterings of Yiddish by old biddies wearing mink coats stepping over bad-off junkies yo sniffing at freaky visions, skinny-ass white kids, shoot the shit, black kids dribbling a basketball, street urchins, they move about in little packs, spread out in the dark, those diaper bandits strike again, dominating the breakaway, the giggle and strut so says a basketball diary.

The Upper West Side, where the nutty lady, laughing at her own mortal soul, intent on finding a verbal solution for her thoughts, searching for what makes the heart leap, searching for decent Chinese food, watching mouthy school kids stuffing their faces with all natural antibiotic hormone free ground chuck burgers pepper jack cheese ranch dressing and chips that's a red hot buffalo slaw on a brioche bun at Five Napkins. I see the dreadful old women, housekeepers, companions, heartless maids pushing wheelchairs containing elderly ladies with legs like skewers, the weak wave of a feather hand and their papery rouged cheeks, no tears in the valleys, yer roots are showing, these painted stares, for no matter one's age, more often than not, a mask covers an obsession with being young again, which I and no one else on the planet will ever be. They say youth is a state of mind but that's hogwash. Just be. Infantile. And fat. And tickle the day.

The famous Zabars on Broadway sells the best in cheese from every corner of the globe. One of the first things my friend and I do in New York, is this charge down Broadway to Zabars cafe and order cheese blintzes with apple sauce from the simple homely crowded with locals, as in elbow to elbow, quick grab that stool, somewhat grubby with crumbs and coffee stains café serving terrible coffee. It is heartening to know that terrible coffee is available everywhere in New York.

The Upper West Side on a clear winter day, shaped by an innocent moon allowing my eyes to keep the blue dazzle of the previous day and a heart beating at my own unpublished crudeness as I browse the bookshops, I can't remember which shops and venerable landmarks, just many people munching pretzels, a symbol for crossed arms or undying love. Is it Lent?

Let us peek into a forgotten hotel lobby, its hush of reveries and pipe-dreams, where the ghosts of impoverished drunk poets writing crystalline rhymes, geniuses chewing on cigars, sour immortals, a bunch of cornballs and in the corner a circle of crusty doyens with beehives, sit on green leather armchairs and begin to gossip. Ozzie's makin' pecan pie, how obscene is Captain Marvel, Gus caught the train to Jersey to hook up with a floozie, Ted gotta a red Cadillac, talk about, yeah small nose, ya know what's coming when yer see, he's gotta little piano, let's order lunch, you wanna Shirley Temple, nope can't afford the Lobster Newberg, we're moving to Boca with Ruthie, did you hear Ida bought a Guinea Pig and she's teaching it to talk well at least say his name Adolph, hey Shorty where you goin, yes sir that's my baby, oh not much to do now but wait out the day.

What dumb sort of mishmash claptrap yacketty yack is this?
Hey it's the yack yack.

silk stocking district

Well alrighty, we venture up to the uppity upness uptown upper classes Upper East Side to the posh spots, the diamond sky, handsome houses furnished with silk furniture, chiffoniers, marble tables, bronzes, cameos, alabaster vases, superior exteriors, yet Brandy's Piano Bar hosts sing-a-longs, a two drink minimum, wear a Batman T-shirt, be prepared to croon old show tunes with Bobby Belfry, order Philly cheese steaks at Shorty's Sports Bar, cheese whizz on everything, three happy hours of Blue Nectar, indulgent lump crab omelets, crepe souffles, shakshuka brunch beauty. There are no angry voices on the Upper East Side, just a herd of rich and comfortable humans, the interminable silk ties, the sharp attire and one of them shouting,

Decide what you wanna do and stick with it.

This feeling of taste, a touch of certainty, the extravagant fear of boredom, great ambition to enlarge a social circle at dinner parties of fine wines and rich food and plenty of hatred.

On the Upper East Side, women using strollers as weapons and the man-eaters, hair the color of popcorn, Botox plumping all the right places, dressing in the latest fashions heading out of Bloomindales, brains the size of peas. Hey big spender put on a happy face, ya got trouble, well anything you can do, I can do better. And then the unceasing scream of a car alarm.

Lexington Avenue paces with a cruel smile, happy to display a fingernail moon on its newly shaved face, a painstakingly exercised streetscape full of complacency, privilege, a messy street and the sharp sensitive eyes of a man-about-town taking in the invading wilderness, a bonfire of traffic, over-demonstrative, on the tacky side in fact, creating instant fatigue, the feeling of blood rushing to my cheeks and a desire to return to a warm apartment as an escape by pretending to be a painter living in a garret, the real bohemian, the avid narcissist, attracted to sad causes, this way of self-importance that more often than not brings tears to the eyes, but instead we tiptoe into Starbucks and order the sweetest ickiest butterscotch latte and think this madness of New York is so worthwhile.

Fifth Avenue ends in discomfort before The Arch of Triumph, a small arch, the woeful arch alone and lamentable and tenuous as a monument, an entry to Washington Square presiding over the buskers and students, the vigilant vegan generation with long confronting beards and peculiar top knots and it's mid-winter here so people are scarce, but we have the graceful snow, the sleet and slosh lifting our spirits.

on observation

An observer obsesses with the observation of the distracting public, as in the hacks, those who lack love or have bad posture, the atheist drunk falling down the stairs at Penn Station, the gabby cab drivers, the woman's face carved from cheap foundation and voices like chalk scraping against the surface of a scream, girls with dreams of poetry, arms covered in flower tattoos, the Garbo women with deep stormy eyes, the old women with amplified assured voices loud like bathwater sucked down a plughole and drab overcoats blowing alongside the gusts.

And after the observing, comes this strenuous attempt at remembering, always the deficient deficit of forgetting follows an occupation of watching and quite often watching other watchers who are not paying attention to what's in front of them, mostly hiding behind dark glasses, hands in pockets, looking over their shoulders in a furtive manner and indulging in the genius of dawdling and memory loss.

The dangers of observation can result in being withdrawn into misunderstandings and confusion, too much scrutiny tires the eyes, overtly staring makes the watcher appear deranged, which is a perfectly fine state to be in while wandering the streets, where I imagine the snow and sleet of winter creates such yearnings of little girls happy to stab old women, teenage boys experimenting with tongue kissing on each other and wives burying husbands in cold graves.

Are you listening to me?

Yes. But I have no idea what in hell you are talking about.

natives

Expansive and garrulous, yet mindful of group etiquette,
the natives, the heart and soul of New York, know the score,
these superstars starring in their own Broadway show, the
straphangers, smart alecks, moochers, gold diggers, the
rubberneckers, herkimer jerkimers and all them apple-
knockers, hey talk the tawk why dontcha?

Native New Yorkers submerged and oblivious to the surrounding
boroughs, always asking me for directions, such is village life.

Start with some men. The uglier the better.

The college scout. The infamous queer, show him the meat
and he'll show you the dollars. The man coming down the
platform at Grand Central. A middle-aged man with a head
like exploding steel wool, perfect skin, delicate plumpness and
absolutely no facial hair. He wears a loud checkered suit. Does
he concern himself with speculations when he looks in the
cupboard at his row of jackets and trousers before choosing
the ugliest outfit on earth? This common species thinks he's
god, probably has a genital deficiency, always takes the stairs
not the escalator that is if stairs are an option and carries a
black plastic bag full of nothing which makes me question,
what tugs at his heart?

A young guy appears in tan loafers teamed with cream pants
and a black jacket, the conservative show-off, not exactly a
dish, in truth he seems bland. I remember there was an era
of wide-eyed actresses calling a man a 'dish'. Which reminds
me that men hate doing the dishes especially if they are a dish.

This particular man hurrying through Tribeca, holds a small blue cardboard box tied with a yellow ribbon. His name is probably Mortimer or Fred, he is not a great conversationalist, but after a couple of whiskies, he's a riot.

Who?

That man running into the Trump building.

A quiet man, deep in thought, dining alone at The Mermaid Inn. He wears his beard under a clean shaven chin, signifying conservatism but also kind of strange. He appears dull and as close to fickle as he can possibly be. And tall with an intelligent face, gray hair freshly trimmed and styled. Of course, he must be a neat freak with a misguided sense of his own importance, because he really is important in the eyes of others, but he doesn't believe he is that important and the word 'pernickety' comes to my mind. His silver spectacles magnify sharp blue eyes, which means he must read The New York Times with a magnifying glass and drink milk with his bread and butter served up by a patient and dedicated spouse brim full of petty fears and worries. I am quite sure he is a ghost. I cannot go on for I am already bored.

The women and girls names can be Sugarplum, Chi Chi, Madison, Lacey bitching about tight buns, astrological signs and how sleazy are bouncers with rings on fat pinkies and strong bladders waving those batons that beat people over the heads in crowds outside bars, somewhere near SoHo, where anorexic women flying the anxiety flag, booking private shopping appointments at J. Crew, walk like lightning, holding onto their pee, avoiding smelly dives and carrying pistols inside their pocketbooks, disappear into office blocks where they keep a lava lamp and a bouquet of tulips on their desks and the boss is a hunky child, wearing an oversized blazer, a funky button-down, sneakers and shield sunglasses making the eyes unreadable and downright spooky.

The physical proof of a punk girl, denim cut-offs close to the crotch, she must be so cold, her socks are pink, she is fine on her own, her face hard with the surface of youth and the loss of fabulousness written on her forehead under blinding red bangs, queen of The Bowery, romper-stomping fat white legs, black kick-ass boots, her nose ring glinting in the rare winter sun. Nose rings make me think of a bull, its nose ring meant to control the animal, to bring it into submission. Is she aware of this?

On the Lower Eastside, the rampage of an afro and gloss lipstick, this young black woman looks like Eartha Kitt, smoking a Camel, trailing a moth eaten fur coat, a pet rat nestling on her shoulder, black Maybelline smudged eyes, rattling her chains, a facial expression of, I'm gonna kick the shit outta you, which is scary and I notice the locals crossing the street to avoid her red pointy stilettos, but still a hard act to follow, the trail of her procession, listening to her shout, *asshole,* at an innocent UPS delivery boy scooting out of the way. I watch her majestical descent into the subway of trapped phantoms, beating against a flow of commuters and I imagine the scream of some poor accountant as she kicks him in the groin. I think I hear the howl of broken promises, of good and evil, of every mythological monster in the world, I think I hear the dead subway air heavy with weeping. I think I hear white men whistling Dixie.

This Irish waitress throws bangers and mash at a bunch of beer bellies downing Hunky Dorys in The Dead Rabbit. And this just does not happen where I come from.

New York natives focus on details, any and every detail, as in the minute specifics, the history, the biological breakdown, the chemical formula, the scientific elements and they do this with an almost heightened and complex anxiety.

Ask a native to describe a glass of water and he or she or whatever begins with the story of how water comes to be, god creating the oceans, the rivers, the lakes and the smallest stream. The native New Yorker goes on and on without drawing breath, going on and off the topic, imagine a catastrophic earthquake, a sensible winter hat, designer glasses, imagine rain against a window, he's the type who drives an SUV, wears authoritarian black with preppy elegance. The character flicking his cigar over and under his tongue. He identifies with power and eroticism.

Pour me a drink.

Club soda? Wawter? Sparkling or still?

And still I say,

Describe a glass of water.

And in New York this temporary confusion. It must be a glass of water, maybe it is not a glass of water. What I know is this. It is a glass of water and I need a stronger drink.

the name rhymes with shoe

My memory worsens. New fears, new defeats, new silences, new losses seem to expand with the waistline. Words for instance fail to materialize. In the apartment building elevator, a heavily pregnant woman asks me,

Your perfume smells fabulous. What's the brand?

I pause for a moment and search my memory, yes a little blue bottle. The scent created by a famous shoe designer.

What is this perfume that I can no longer smell? Far too much sprayed on my wrists and neck, hoping the scent might help me fill the vacant spaces, the rooms, the shopping malls, the emptiness leaving a trail of everything, nope can't remember.

You know I just can't remember. The name rhymes with shoe.

She smiles, both hands on her huge belly.

Jimmy Choo?

That's it.

I should be polite and ask her when the baby is due. But my brain ticks backwards. My brain boards a sinking ship and sails across the Hudson to a Manhattan shore, maroons me so happy on this island that also seems pregnant. Just don't inform the pregnant woman how memory disintegrates with age and from giving birth. Ping goes the elevator. The woman says,

Have a nice day.

And I chime with my best chimes,

You have a nice day too.

And she waddles off into the great face of cheeky Manhattan, the immense collective presence, this bristling expanse, a monstrous organism surrounded by rivers, the sea and at the helm, a woman waving a flaming torch. A city of indomitable power that rushes and shrieks like a manic elaborate dance lit with a battle between joy, desperation, defiance and the giant dancer, a steel and concrete machine with colossal jaws and fists punching the low sky wincing from the ceaseless audacity of its towers with spines as straight as javelins. These money skyscrapers pregnant with permanence, stifling visibility. This lateral thinking sideways of uptown, midtown, downtown, the looming, the magnitude, the bearing down.

to the max

In search of a hair straightener, I take the steep escalator down into the bowels of the wonder that is T J Maxx, a dangerous place owning a cult mentality, the thrill of the hunt, the prices are a steal, the place to buy stuff you don't need with money you don't have, ultimate retail, the perfect way to cure a nervous breakdown. But I am uncertain if they have electrical appliances. After filling a shopping cart with thirty items of clothing, sunglasses, scarves, hats, shower curtains, a thousand thread count king size bedsheets, blankets, picture frames and a whole new world perspective for a total of about fifty dollars, a shop assistant approaches me. Her flashing white teeth, white lipstick, heavily mascaraed eyes, menacing jewelry and tattooed eyeliner more than frightening, but then horror oh my god, the woman has huge ringlets like blonde sausages covering her scalp. Each ringlet lies in symmetrical rows like a lithograph of Percy Bysshe Shelley. Yikes I can't ask her if the store stocks hair straighteners. I freeze. Her briskness and bracelets rattle with impatience. I gather my many shocks and put on a serious expression and ask,

Do you stock any small appliances?

Her bracelets light up and she jangles her heady coils.

What are you looking for?

An electric kettle.

Well, honey, I'm sorry we don't carry kettles. You could try Duane Reade, the drugstore. You'll find one on almost every block. In fact, there is one right across the road from here.

As I unload the cart, the cashier asks me,

Have you found everything you were looking for?

Well not really, for a start, I wasn't looking for any of this.

On my way to Duane Reade, I notice a wrinkled sign hanging on a wire fence outside a school. Opportunity Tarts Now. The 'S' quite hidden in the bend of a crease. Damn it. This reminds me to buy something sweet for my friend. I should have bought that packet of key lime flavored, chocolate dipped, coconut whipped, butter caramel, hazelnut cookies from T J Maxx.

listen pal

My friend and I borrow this precious and immense city carefully revealed, cornices attach to facades, right at our fingertips tapping gently, say hi it's a wonderful day, have a wonderful life. It's wonderful to walk past the pond in Central Park where two hundred and seventy-five species of birds live.

We walk blocks and blocks to Columbia University built on the site of an old lunatic asylum and now the trees strung with fairy lights create magic and peace from a history of lunacy, of waking up on the edge of an iron bed, the city grows as distortion and revelation into the open eyes of the insane.

Let's go in the other direction, the long way, be quick about it, do not come to a staggering halt thinking of a city deaf to mountains, passing these compressed communities inside apartment blocks steeped in an insulated un-world, the occasional jumpers, the incurable eccentrics, the failed actors and singers performing at Bar Thalia on open mic night.

We reach 72nd Street, famous for slaughter. The Dakota Building remembers Lennon lying on the footpath, his last breath under the gas lamps burning real flames. The Dakota Indian, searching for a reason, fitting inside the hole in time when Lennon fell. Blood on the pavement. *Imagine all the people.* His last words, *yes I am*

What about the plays, the cabarets, the ballet, the opera? What are we doing now? Let me just say, my friend and I reach the unappealing Lincoln Square, an aloof fortress of performing arts with a somewhat hysterical fountain. I suppose it's okay, I'll come back to this for the opera, the ballet, the furs, the unbelievable price of a flute of softly spoken champagne in the lobby at interval, yes come back to this one fine evening, wearing my butterfly broach and the neon city and of course warm clothes.

We cross Broadway to a place where the world globe spins in the middle of Columbus Circle, participating in the dream of Manhattan, making an effort to capture the sense of great times and tall deeds of this city. Let New York tell me her story. The spectacle of long-winded avenues from block to block, corners of brazen cross streets, the buildings in pursuit of distinction and style and awe. The assertive and proud New Yorkers, the occasional crazy fuckers talking to themselves, pushing all the mysteries and spirits out of the way.

Picture the mystery of a deli, its harsh fluorescent lights, the sneezed-on salad bars, the weird orange cheese, kind of a museum of sandwiches.

And the literary exploits of Dylan Thomas, on a moonless night at his favorite bar, The White Horse Tavern, which I visit on my first trip and the bar is full of fresh-faced young men wearing tuxedos, I guess hail from New Jersey. I sit alone and wonder at these small men soft as a cow's tongue, their milk fed faces and ears deaf to stars falling. Only I can see and hear the blind hearty and blank eyes and white linking arms and the rise and fall of the boys are back in town, Friday night they'll be dressed to kill. And I am the first to drown when I hear Dylan Thomas has gone back to the Chelsea where his face turns blue and on the run to his grave, he says, I've finally found something on earth to live for.

I swear that bloke with the dome-like forehead, black beard and glasses is Alan Ginsberg, how I imagine a Jewish professor to look, maybe with the addition of a top hat and an opera scarf and a friendly smile. But really, Ginsberg is a Buddhist rocking and rolling arrogant gibberish human animal with the earth going round and round inside his eyeballs as he writes stacked entities with a blowtorch and cries, don't hide the madness. But I think hiding is much easier and blowtorches are dangerous.

The swarms of humanity, a hearty shadow of history casting itself over the architecture, street signs, and corner cafes. How to delve, absorb, dig into this amassed metropolis. This impenetrable enigma of duded-up stone and stoops. The car exhaust, the garbage, the smell of money enough to buy me a soda.

The cab driver, a version of urban detachment, a living man, his presence obscure to passengers entering his taxicab. And once directions are given, the man condemned to no mans' land, to a nonexistence, as faceless as the streets, the river, the deadly gray of concrete and the absence of light. We get into a cab, a yellow Plymouth, the Indian driver looks scared from behind the bullet proof glass in place to protect the tiny statue of Ganesha on the dash. Honk honk. The cabbie glances nervously in the mirror as he turns into Christopher Street. I am sure once he hears our accents he will relax.

On the back of his seat, in front of my face, a small television screen shows a stream of type announcing the breaking news. *Early this morning a falling air conditioner hit a woman on the head.*

Christ.

The leaking pipe of anxiety. Bad news brings terror to the irrational mind. I think of the number of air conditioners balancing precariously outside the windows of New York apartment buildings. Millions and millions. Yet the NYPD claims, death by air conditioner is a rare occurrence.

I don't believe that.

You worry too much.

Even so I keep close to the curb, making my way through icy slush piles beside parked cars snug under snow. Rows and rows of frozen sedans, station wagons and SUV's. These undefined pudding shapes, plump mounds, giant lumps, sometimes doubling as refrigerators for those living in confined spaces. I must forget about the possibility of falling air conditioners. For the life of ideas is the only one worth living.

So take us to all the speakeasies. The Dizzy Club. One of the dives on Fifty-Second Street. Its motto, 'A rolling tomato gathers no mayonnaise'. Do they call mayonnaise 'mayo' here? The dizzy drinkers slip on the slippery mayo streets.

The mirror behind the bar reflects and multiplies all the spirits, the labels, Mescal, Hennessy, Bombay Sapphire, the plumping of patrons faces, the plumbing, the plastic surgery, the tummy tucks, the boozy comfort, one dollar for the remarkable oysters, two cocktails for the price of one. The first sip, a second, a third to make us relax, no one cares about our wacky wobble.

Is it me or is it you?

It's both of us. Our reflection in the omnipresent mirror imagines our brilliant chatter, quoting white male poets, Auden, Lowry, Ginsberg, the tangle of them, of their talent and what are the current terms for ethnicity, gender and race? Immeasurable, not fixed but rather fluid and imprecise. The incredible multi-ethnic population of New York. Another miracle. The diversity. The volcanic energy. The colors of another sunset.

Toothpicks at the ready, a tumbler of plastic straws, lemons, salt, green olives and a sticky cash register cha ching. Have I tried acid? No. Have I left the planet? Have I been in a train wreck? Never. Do you remember the green beaded curtains and that spooky clairvoyant? Do I have a personal guru? My friend says,

You've had too much to drink.

A man sits on a barstool and shakes while deep in conversation with a vacant chair. The song-lines on his headache face, prehistoric rock carvings of a drinker, a melancholic, a sailor, a failure. The enthralling ruin of himself telling the barman to put ninety proof on his slate. A whole bottle of Cognac writes his poetry. Poor old Auden. The martini moon pours another with a twist. The scary words.

Listen pal, we reserve the right to refuse anyone.
Can mindfulness reinvent humanity?

What is right in the bright night of the heart?

I will not be as others are I will not see as others see.

I am the odd one. Excessive, operatic, erratic exaggerations like a sniveling soprano. So many odd things. The odd fussing. The odd writing on the wall. The odd off chance. The odd bottle stashed in a window box blooming with red geraniums. The odd nip to steady the nerves. A forest of oddities creates fresh air, enough wind to stitch up the starchy farts, the stiff necks dropping dead in their parsimonious thinking that they are above it all. What, I think, is above and below at least something I just cannot think what. My brain hums with oddities. My heart belongs in this wonderland of growth against many odds. The odd hours. The odd jobs. The odd and precious days. Of oddity growing, of the odd me surviving in spite of all my oddness. My friend and I are both odd within our separate long panics, in separate oceans, lacking eloquence, two bumblers, two fuck ups yet docile with sore feet wandering about in a sophisticated city.

And I save napkins from diners, also the tiny paper packets of salt and pepper because don't even ask about money, honey. This year the Australian dollar is sixty-two cents to the American dollar. I sing, we're in the money. He says,

You've got it back to front. We're paying almost double for everything.

Which makes Uncle Toby's oatmeal over seven dollars a box. And we can't afford tiramisu. Welcome to my life. A breakfast of expensive porridge refuses to dampen our rant and gallop. We gush out into the up and down streets, careful of the wet pavements, swinging happiness and bouncy carefree like a bright lantern and worrying about that surreal moment of calculating a tip.

the anthill

That is Wall Street, the stock exchange, a temple of fortune, the terminal of money, greed, throw them coins high in the air, roll them silver dollars into many pockets, this lure of easy money to buy useless and expensive things, the gamble, the inside rumors, sometimes transforming into a monstrous collective panic, a place I decide to never visit.

pure blizzardry

The soundless walk in a city dreaming about itself, hiding behind a pale but inscrutable curtain. Bring down the curtains, bring down the ethereal snow, the falling quiet and all week the disappearing sky and the promise of happiness.

The blue van parked just off Seventh Avenue in Times Square. The sign on the van advertises, Mr Rooter the plumber, like no other plumber. I wish him here in the flesh, to see if he lives up to his name, not in *that* way. Is Mr Rooter an attractive plumber? Does he keep his hands clean? Why is he like no other plumber? What does it mean to be like no other plumber? He might dance and sing love songs while he installs toilet cisterns. His spanner technique could be superior and original. I am wise to this now. I don't believe that's his real name.

Gawd, it's a mean blizzard today. An impenetrable vortex. The poet, Alexander Blok describes a blizzard as calm and light. This blizzard is not calm and light, this blizzard is Russian and epic. I picture an official in a badger fur coat, pince-nez on his nose, threatening sabotage. I am wishing for a sled-mobile, a fox-fur hat with ear flaps. Times Square is not as crowded in a blizzard and a rare choice for our outing, but we are a rare and special species like Mr Rooter.

A distinctive day for the blizzard wizard, I see a snow vision, the famous Herculean man with long blonde hair, the naked cowboy with perfect biceps a six-pack torso, meaning he must bench press. Today apparently as always, he is wearing only white Y-fronts, nowhere to hide his gun, white cowboy boots, a huge white cowboy hat with a rhinestone band and he's waving a guitar like a snow angel. Give him wings. He is running through the stars and stripes, through snow banks and snowfall on Forty Second Street. A magical man heading for heaven, leaping into a limousine and I think street performance must be quite lucrative.

In reality his name is Burck. He is a Trump supporter. The cowboy hat and his face are small and wrinkled. He looks like one of the contestants on Master Chef and once he got arrested during Bike Week for panhandling in Daytona, Florida. There must have been a scuffle because his guitar got broken. According to the local news on Orlando.com, he was booked into Volusia County Jail. It seems they don't say incarcerated any more.

As we continue the battle of the blizzard, a woman stops us and asks if we want to be part of the audience for The Late Show hosted by David Letterman, taped live in The Ed Sullivan Theatre. Of course I say yes and he says what and we enter a different kind of vortex that is free tickets. Queuing for three hours, the many and detailed rules, no hats, no calling out, no heckling and when a woman in the seat in front of us shouts something, the usher grabs her by the arm and hauls her out of the theatre. Brutal, I think, the show isn't that great. A better episode was aired in 2009, when Madonna, smoking a fat cigar, calls Letterman a sick fuck, gives him a pair of her underpants and asks, aren't you going to smell them? She says 'fuck' about seventeen times, informs the audience that Letterman kisses up to his guests and recommends peeing in the shower to cure athletes foot. I think she is fabulous and stoned. The audience hates her. Today the show is slick as ice, with humorous monologue, diminutive banter, skits, bizarre conceptual stunts and a smooth David Letterman, the robot with a permanent grin pasted onto his jollification, thank god The Ed Sullivan Theatre is beautiful.

please swipe again

There is the astonishing velocity of most New Yorkers to be patient with non-New Yorkers.

Do you know a slice of pizza costs the same as a subway ticket?

My friend swipes his Metro Card at the barred turnstile, one of only two turnstiles at Bryant Park Station. A message flashes, INSUFFICIENT FUNDS.
He fumbles and swipes his Metro Card too slow, resulting in the message,

SWIPE AGAIN AT THIS TURNSTILE
or *PLEASE SEE AGENT*
or *PLEASE SWIPE AGAIN.*

He has swiped again. There is no agent. The machine deducts the fare but does not wave the passenger through. He tries another swipe. The message *JUST USED. THE TURNSTILE IS SICK AND TIRED. YOUR CARD SMELLS. KEEP SWIPING UNTIL A FURIOUS RABBLE GATHERS BEHIND YOU.* Arggh.

There exist many varieties of swipes. The cocky swipe, the running swipe, the long reach swipe, the idiot swipe, the poetic swipe, the caffeine swipe, and the sure swipe, the momentarily illuminated by the saints swipe, the Virgin Mary swipe and the unscheduled second coming swipe.

My turnstile blinks GO. Great. I push through to the other side. He swipes again. JUST USED.

What are you doing?

My friend keeps swiping. The frenzied swipe. The exasperated swipe. I tell him,

Try the other turnstile.

In the depths of the tunnel leading to the platform, a busker plays a familiar tune on his trumpet. It's A Wonderful World.

Why does this always happen to you? Try it again.

A commuter approaches my friend. The commuter appears pale and exhausted, world weary, a sad life maybe. The commuter advises,

You either have to buy another fare or wait fifteen minutes and swipe again.

My friend is now purple-faced and speechless with rage, he stands for a full two minutes staring uncomprehendingly at the concerned commuter who now looks worried.

Do you understand me? Do you want me to speak in Spanish?
My friend crashes back to earth and thanks the man, who continues on his not so merry way. There is no ticket office here. My friend shuffles the notes in his wallet as if waiting for an explosion. I notice a magician with lovely dreadlocks watching us. I whisper,

For God's sake put your money away.

This tiny choreography of caution and patience, me always on the other side, ready to go and laughing as hard as an hysterical cockatoo flying downhill into a field of dead daffodils. My friend is too fat to leap over the turnstile. The fleeting silence. The deafening purr of footsteps. The eternal dimness. The dirty tiles. My feet hurt. We are off the map, off our heads. This undergoing of symbolic changes underground. This trap dreaming of hot dogs, of winding back the clock, of petty squabbles about not eating poultry, about owning too much crap. How outlet stores make me want to fart. We wait for fifteen minutes. Times up. He swipes his card. INSUFFICIENT FUNDS. Fuuuuuck. The distant sound of long melodic notes soar from the busker's trumpet, *It's A Wonderful Life.* But only if you can swipe the correct swipe.

snapshots

The passing pigeons, too numerous, too vague, too random and without a brolly, oblivious to the rain that wets their wings, these birds have a better view of the city from the bridge.

Smoked pigeon, torched eel and dancing shrimp make a hearty addition to a multidimensional Manhattan with its bittersweet undertones and why not plop in a cherry with a stalk creating a real ole man-drink.

Through crowded Macy's, my friend carries his new umbrella horizontally under his arm, skewering innocent Americans.

The temptation of fast, of flat out, don't slip on that penny for hope is a lone violin rendering the loneliness of music.

The consciousness of how embarrassing, when New Yorkers stuck in a long queue, moan softly at the sight of a short Australian woman at the counter in Century 21. I empty a pile of loose change from my wallet onto a counter.

Is this a quarter or a dime?

The surprise of a downpour, a connection, the big soak, noticing a fast volume of physical movement, hurry the sum of lines and the one minute it takes to swallow a bagel, get here as soon as possible, which means rush the tunnel of now.

My friend stops suddenly on congested West 34th Street and five rushing commuters slam into the back of him. In Times

Square, he pauses on 7th Avenue and a small queue begins to form behind him. I drag him away.

You have got to keep moving.

What if we behave like characters in novels? Innocents aging. Shall we appear at a fashionable hour? Can we agitate society? Be vulgar? What if I drive a carriage up Fifth Avenue? Are we like patterns stenciled on wallpaper? Shall we strike out for ourselves? Be original? I laugh softly under a Chantilly veil, my hands encased in an ermine muff, for we are cartoons, nothing but cartoons.

Do you know cave-fish and city-dwellers have ceased to develop eyes because they have no use for them? How do we avoid the bores, the snobs, the overbearing knobs? My friend stops listening.

Are you listening? What do you want to do? Hell's Kitchen for a haircut by a swish stylist? What does bare-bones aesthetic mean? Who murdered the landlady? I hear the portentous beatings of drum. I see a chorus line of bobble-headed tap dancers, disappearing into the park. He says,

Let's go to the park.

In the park, we find the occasional frightened maple or oak, not sure which, oak or maple, walking the Mall full of show-offs in their finery, well mostly European tourists wearing elegant scarves and bomber jackets.

Snow defines the leafless trees by resting on each black branch, vanilla frosting on chocolate.

On a dull day, the naive sky washes whiter than white, highlighting strips of ice, which I fancy to be idealistic, the opposite of quicksand. And I think feral squirrels are like feathers or light lint. I can't decide. Feathers are pretty, lint is horrible.

Inside the apartment, I often stand a few feet back from the window, then I hold up my hand and measure the width of the New York skyline between my forefinger and thumb. Its not so big anymore.

Always moving away from the window ledge. Not too far, stay close enough to see the park. The theatre of melting snow. We watch the disappearance of one scene give way to the next. Winter sucks the life from subtle hues fading to gray, an unhurried process revealing a naked park, a gaunt park with a parched face, kind of fragility, making urinating dogs nervous. A tired park laying its' heart bare. This blunt abstraction apologizing for how cold the park has become. The pond's sheen remains unbroken like the steel of denser sentiments, what lies beneath, when will the cracks show, who will go under. Beside the pond, a delicate lyricism of willows the color of pollen, weeping over unforgiving ice. This park, in limbo, buds in production, birds nesting, activities of renewal hidden from me, as I look down from the seventeenth floor, just not looking all the way down, giddy from the suction power of height, thinking thoughts of steel limbo, a weeper at beauty, these contemplations of the mind, the thirst for fat sensibilities in the mood for tea and cake.

The equivalent to Angel Food Cake in Australia is called a Sponge Cake, not the prettiest name and the American chocolate version of Angel Food Cake is called Devil's Food Cake. Our chocolate version is Mud Cake. Mud and sponge, how in god's name did that happen? Mud is dull, filthy and rhymes with thud and dud. Sponges must be squeezed of all liquids, they are inert and if a sponge was an animal it would take the form of a sloth. A sponge is the worst type of beige, it's basically not worth talking about. Angel Food Cake and Devil's Food Cake sound like a whimsical fairy story and both those names make perfect sense. My friend and I buy Angel Food Cake (one hundred and ninety calories per serving) from the Whole Foods Market and this particular version is not that great. The truth of the ingredients, egg whites, water, guar gum, sodium citrate, triethyl citrate, sugar, wheat flour, sea salt, cream of tartar, vanilla flavor, water, glycerin, alcohol, caramel color, vanilla extract, organic guar gum and organic xanthan gum. There is a notable absence of butter. The secret to the lightness as in the molecular and fundamental configuration is the egg whites beaten until stiff which sounds like murder. But beating the ovalbumin and globulins creates the aerated texture of foam. And the cake is not at all diabetic friendly. Without frosting, the cake is dry and tasteless. This is disappointing, Angel Food Cake is supposed to be abnormally light, a pale cake without fat, baked in a ring shape and covered with soft icing. It is supposed to be weightless. It is meant to defy gravity. It must be the kind of cake an angel eats. I can safely claim that angels would not eat the Whole Foods Market Angel Food Cake. Do you believe in angels? Do you know that angels are without gender? Angels are the lowest in the celestial hierarchy. But angels are superior to humans in intelligence and power. Angels are invisible, which is why it's difficult to prove they exist. Humans are visible only on the outside. We cannot see through each other. I assume angels are capable of seeing through each other. Which is lucky and doesn't that just take the cake?

On rare afternoons, the setting sun illuminates one side of every visible building in New York. Geometric high-rises of light and shade below a monster cloud like a zeppelin hovering the length of the skyline as the sky slowly yellows, or shall I say is yellowing, or turns yellow either way the sky is always right. And the sky is always in the same place which is comforting, not like me going completely off the topic.

High-rises declare the potency of Man. And these buildings, like man, grope the sky and ask the right questions and make declarations that are mostly ignored.

Skyscrapers are blind. They ignore the little people running around and into and up them. Skyscrapers are blind on purpose, for it is not necessary for a skyscraper to be able to see what is in front of them, which is usually another wall of glass and steel, that being an even taller skyscraper. Some skyscrapers are torn down. This is called demolition, so it is not wise to become emotionally invested in any one particular tall building, especially those that are rusty, the aging skyscrapers if there are any, are not pleasant, not quite ugly, they are just there taking up the sky space, like people sporting a breezy confidence.

The city aches with feeling, it's as high as possible and strutting in order to be bright, crisp, emphatic, lording over the gnomes, some only just surviving, some disappearing, some asking what ever happened to Fairy Soap? Five cents a cake in the shape of an oval, advertised as pure, white, floating and a picture of a little girl asking, have you a little fairy in your home? Imagine the furor about that.

Let's buy a barrel of hooch. *What?* We call it grog. Either name is acceptable and cute, though when I think about it, grog possesses the connotation of a groggy grinch-like creature rubbing its eyes and wondering what the fuss is all about and wishing for more of everything especially sleep, groggy is how I feel after too much hooch and hooch is a cuter name. By a long shot.

Do they say long shot here? No, they say, take aim.

Picture the city as this fascinating, slightly loopy, reincarnation of the sad-eyed lady of the lowlands, tiptoeing through the crystal ice, pretending to be disarming and as pungent as a pineapple. This is energy and potency, a gifted and tormented character from the isle of joy. The sad-eyed lady of the lowlands writes using precise cursive lettering, a talent called penmanship, this insertion of man into every word and she prints her own money from anything that resembles tenderness or death.

On a Chelsea gallery crawl, a black limousine with tinted windows stops outside the Gagosian, a difficult word to pronounce, if only art could talk, the meticulous faking it, the cumulative stupor, the gravitas sinking in a vat of pink foam. The car waits for no man. The car slithers away to the big nothings and many somethings and unlikely phobias all in previews once upon a New York hello fiddling on the roof of above and beyond, of bed, bath and beyond.

The city indulges in emotional yelping, honking neighborhoods, beating the crossing lights, ignoring the red light, let the go light shine on the scrapes of fading posters, who here carries a flashlight, a knife or a gun? Just the rats in the subway, the occasional cockroach nosing about in Chinatown. Ginsberg called New York a hopeless city of idiots, but underneath I know it hides a sacred steel brain with traction. And I am lucky, having never been mugged, for I never go any place where there is the possibility of a mugging. I go to surreal places in my mind and now I am remembering the cross streets uptown, the Gothic and Queen and Byzantine town houses. Once I was walking with Charlotte and Diego, how they stopped in wonderment at the beauty of this architecture. I guess I am used to it now. But we still come back year after year, avoiding the spiky green statue taking in the postcard views.

Look out the window! The cold and glorious and the lack of sailboats. In this café, we are sitting beside yet another pole, a bottle of Tabasco in the place where he took my hand and happy heart hearts me.

Mussels eggs and poetry, it's raining screaming flies nothing better I think, oh yes the wind whistles its dog, tomorrow the coolness of the gallows, dreaming of the alphabet discovering Marcel Broodthaers, Alchemist of The Avante-Garde at MoMA with Viviane and Gerald.

Here we are, says Daniele, The sun will come out this afternoon and Central Park will be magical.

Edith Wharton wrote The Age Of Innocence in a stark stone four level building with pine trees on the roof and Weight Watchers at ground level.

Just up the road soldiers are singing and marching along Fifth Avenue past the library these war shadows on a sunny day do not sing tra lah lah.

Watching an anti-Trump march, give them all the thumbs up.

The sign at Union Square Market that says, Eggs Are Not Dairy.

Tonight the streets of New York are invaded by hundreds of Santa Clauses, which is a good thing right? Most of the Santa Clauses are drinking in bars and the rest are planning which bars to go for a drink. It is Christmas only in New York, the mile high tourists are piling up, the lights are brighter than bright, the glitz, the bells, the tree, Fifth Avenue all on steroids, the song, Do They Know It's Christmas on replay in my brain and down near Union Square at Pete's Tavern, surviving the prohibition, often blessed by the clergy, notorious for the highest number of bar-babies conceived by would-be parents, where O Henry went into voluntary liquidation with a weeks' wages and penned Gift of The Magi, where the barman stutters tongue-tied and scarlet, my friend and I are greeted by Santa Clause's donkey wearing Bavarian lederhosen and bells and a spiffy Santa hat. We give him or her or whatever a pat, the donkey snorts and shivers in the very particular way that a donkey shivers. We head inside to the warmth of history, the jovial incandescence, to sit in a black lacquer booth and drink a festive eggnog with golden brandy seeming to hold sunshine a prisoner within its auriferous depths. Pity the poor donkey outside in the cold.

East village gets us blue grass banjos, butterflies, glitter walls, say no thanks to a fish bowl margarita, it's time to meet us in Coney Island Baby.

Let us walk to the places we never walk to.

Yes. I am the Trivia Goddess. Trivia is exact.

Souvenirs are perplexing and unexceptional.

New York is the only one for me.

the long nothing

Freedom is a drab March sun warming the animals pacing and pacing confined against their will, right or wrong, not to welcome the spring with a visit to Central Park Zoo, waking our why questions. What have the animals done to deserve the incarceration of long scarce? Pacing and pacing. There is nothing else for the prisoners to do while humans snack, drink, joke and point at them.

Constraint is a shackle, is a defeat of a tall pink bird with a metal ring around its ankle. Do we mistake it for a flamingo? The bird extends its beak and grabs a tortoise by the leg. The tortoise makes a break for it and escapes, not from the zoo though. Then the flamingo's short attention span picks a fight with a bird, too small to be a peacock.

Inside this chain, this unsettling show of energy, the long nothing, the whole longing time, animals in captivity. Wrong is the right to call them dumb animals, free from their own confusion. This history of objectification long, and long the imprisonment trap of ceaseless tedium, brain dead, endless days, don't mistake it for a life. And the crime is the cruelty of human fascination with the caged exotic.

The true sighting of an unfamiliar black and white creature sleeping on a large rock, peaceful in the long nothing, hairy sluggish, it wakes for a moment, lapses, opens yellow bleary eyes, not beautiful and I cringe at this solitary confinement of yes, the creature observes everything, the creature is static, but the longing breaks a heart the shape of the same as before, then drops into sleep.

And the gorilla frowns at what he cannot see. Come and look children. The fur, the bugs, the civilized garden of resignation. Let go. Don't fight it. There is no single nothing, but to remain inert, sleep and dream, pace and pace. Even the simple raccoon prefers gorgeous freedom, swishing a striped tail and sniffing busily, scratching at a tree trunk. A tragic rope hangs from a branch inviting the racoon to take a swing at oblivion.

I suppose that pile of white painted boulders in the polar bear's habitat is meant to trick the bears into thinking they are at home in the North Pole. Oh come on. Do you think you can fool a polar bear? Don't hesitate the sad leaving, the chosen daydreaming of a better life. Remember the glorious moment of her birth? Now the polar bear lives in defeat, unable to protest.

But for the delight of children in awe, assembling for a photo opportunity in front the otter tank. Otter faces press against the glass, which is acceptable to these four chubby children standing in a row. The father says,

Scooch in.

Two of the girls hold balloons in the shape of hearts in front of their faces. They lean in close, squashing the littlest boy between them. The biggest boy stands behind and hunches over, holding up two fingers in a V shape. Peace sign. The father crouches down and grins showing all his teeth. As freedom is a gone photo, the big smiles. The complete hope for these camera faces at a zoo built for the children's pleasure.

I hope a magician comes in the middle of the night and unlocks the cages, here is the key, come and go as you please and now beside the corny tear-jerking normal, is a freed wind-swept polar bear ice-skating on the frozen pond in Central Park. She is as free as the emancipated child ordering a slice, extra cheese to go, say cheese.

we never shimmy or have fireside chats

But, yes even so, my friend and I walk the High Line, where the stereotypes walk, the glory line, the working line of a romantic elevated once neglected freight rail line, quite historic enough, becomes a hybrid public space between West 34th Street and Gansevoort Street, now we know how to transform industrial infrastructure into a beautiful day out, pizza, ice cream, beetroot smoothie, doughnuts. Be our new friend, loving the tender plantings of a higher line, loving those citified chic tourists walking the line, picture them using the swanky readymade background for selfies, keep a rush-less tempo no hurry here. Measure the many of crowds and narrow. Are we sheep again? All facing the same direction, strolling past the frequent exit points, and the long plentiful grasses appear sweet and unfussy and make me want to get high. What's all the fuss about?

And close to the High Line, I notice a large billboard advertising storage spaces, a forgettable image of a box or warehouse or box inside a warehouse, a small splash of blood red, of course blood is my interpretation. The billboard's caption is absolute absurdity to me, it makes no sense and seems to be more of a warning in great gawping goliath letters. *Until It's Safe To Have A Tea Party Again.* Safe from what?

After glasses of wine at a downtown bar near the High Line, I see more of the more signs in the city, it's a sign from no it isn't and losing our way under a bright yellow sign sighted on the railing of a bridge. Are there bridges in Chelsea?

Reality defines the masses at home tucked up in their one thousand thread count sheets, they mistake sleep for a condition, a refraction of telling the reality, come back to the sign on the railing of a bridge reads futility, *The sooner you park your car the sooner you can stop thinking about parking your car.* Wordiness appeals to the inevitable retaining a secret sense, a sort of neurosis happening here, putting everyone under pressure, a strange proverb in the color of a watchword puce. This underlying fear among the native grasses as seen from the low grasses. And in the distance, I can see a grey warship floating on the Hudson.

The overcoat problem is complicated by arms inside the wrong sleeves. I spin and swap inside out, strangling myself with my scarf and outside, slip and stumble in the wintery weather.

My skirt is too tight.

Hold my arm.

Only affably tipsy and humming, waiting for an hour to pee, astronaut love returns the same, but so different, give me winter wine, that old familiar line, a slave to the demon drink, says the kinks, there's whiskey in the jar, home brew, moonshine, give me a heap whole zing, get caught in the rain, right the train. Where will we, oops.

My friend and I drop into the rabbit hole subway wobble also and us cheering the effortless slide of our Metro Cards, heads down, rather expert now sweeping through the magical turnstiles and the C train gut-rocking carriages of the blue line reptile swallowing us, tottering a vacant seat of orange and puke yellow, too bright, blinding in fact and deafening, just what I need at this point in pissed time, metal on metal wheels, voracious screeching at fleeting plastic humans, one verging on nausea, speeding through, the train ghost rears up roaring.

This is my train.

Nothing more, but this declaration of ownership, an admonishment. Are we trespassers? Have we crossed a boundary? Any ghost can claim ownership through honest means. But first a ghost must own itself. The train ghost roars.

I don't understand.

Fine. A stupid ghost. Also sober and ugly.

Strangers on a train so strange, the woman wearing a coat, vampish girls quite beaded and static, staring at I-Phones, a couple of Texans screaming in whispers at each other about some sort of horror, like finding a rat's tail in the broth. In the seat opposite us, sits the exact opposite of tantalizing, a stoner ogre slumps half asleep, legs sprawled, a claw hammer poking out of his pocket.

I don't see him coming until he lands on me. Not the bloke with the claw hammer, not the train ghost, but the fattest man in the entire universe. He rushes into the carriage at Ninetieth Street and plops on the vacant seat beside me, engulfing me in a tsunami of blubber and crushing me against the chrome rail at the end of the row of seats. On the other side of the fat guy, a girl in a red dress catapults up like a streak of lava. This guy is oblivious to my dazed surrender. Swimmy in the brain of worry, drowning in flab. My strap hanger friend reaches over and drags me out from under the blob. Gawd almighty. My mascara running all over my blur and where's my hat? Is it wrong to complain about obese people? The prevalence, the complications, the risk factors, a morbidly obese BMI. The only cure is to stop eating. I promise I will never eat pork again.

The train is crowded, we cram ourselves into the standing area. I don't know if the standing area beside the door has a particular name, but I call it the standing area. At the next stop, a woman and a boy squash into the carriage. It is not obvious at first that the boy is mentally challenged, that is until without warning he screams like a trapped animal, the sound is so sudden and so close that there seems to be a collective flinch of terror and the bloke standing next to me appears to be on the verge of heart failure, still nobody moves, so much hardiness in the soul, all the fear is in the eyes.

Tiny hangover cure at the Metro Diner, this art deco masterpiece, its neon panels wrap around the corner of 100th and Broadway. High above the counter, a line of red and silver metallic circles each containing an individual letter, spells out FRESH & DELICIOUS. Which I am far from feeling, hanging my coat on the handy hook and sliding into a glass-partitioned booth with comforting leather seats. Two choices of coffee, leaded or unleaded, the antsy waiter fills our mugs and brings us an enormous wedge of carrot cake with a mountain of whipped cream, even the crumbs are huge, and nestled in the cream cheese frosting, I find a perfectly formed orange carrot made of sugar complete with a tiny green leaf. The cake appears to be fresh and delicious, but it isn't. Anyway, we keep going back to the Metro Diner for the eggs and the ambiance.

Strangler Broadway dashes with secret urban lives, a certain psychosis, a world of fantasy names, the Rue of Roues, Golden Gulch, Fraudway, Tungsten Territory, Via Lobsteria, Beer Gulch, The Illuminated Thoroughfare.

My friend and I go to Zabars to buy cheese. The small crowded historic store, holy grail of foodie heaven with narrow aisles and olives marinating in barrels opposite an embankment of cheeses. We are careful not to bump into the affluent customers, this well-heeled crowd of worldly intellectuals, celebrities, tourists and housewives from New Jersey.

In the deli section, there are blood stains on the white aprons worn by stout male shop assistants sharpening knives, steel on steel and expertly slicing brisket, wrapping foie gras before offering a choice of hams. Spiral, skinless, shankless? But no touching. Maybe a taste.

Under a glass counter, a silent choir of pickled lox, salt-belly lox, hand sliced nova, sturgeon, hot-smoked kippered salmon, Scottish cured salmon, pastrami salmon, gravlax and caviar and I just want to lie down and push it all into my face.

Oops sorry my trolley rams into a blond Russian woman drooling over the meals-to-go counter. Flecks of cheap black mascara cling to her eyelashes. Her face maps veins and wrinkles and moles and huge nostrils. She stabs a chubby finger at the paella and grunts. I hear her hunger.

Next aisle, at the bakery counter, the long queue coils around to the grocery section. The air hums with the sumptuous aromas of fresh baked challah, bagels, croissants, poetic coffee beans and inflagrante molto delizioso raspberry cinnamon rugelach, beautiful this necessity for patience and tolerance creates New York as a phenomenon of a world united and successfully compressed in all life and all races.

In New York, I never experience the audacity to converse on literary giants who write playful avant-garde postmodern stuff, like the running shoe (?) like warrior princes, fierce pirates, the reverence for logic, the disdain for superstition and as for literary giants, it's a pity they are all men which means someone does their laundry, their taxes and generally helps out. Yes. I have just been to Barnes & Noble.

A female writer's abundance of originality and fluency of style survives her sanity and her inventive ripening appears to be liberated from the potency of sense. So there, but of course I always fall back into incoherency.

The perfect Friday late afternoon downtown, losing an earring, a black fabric flower, a cheap earring I bought at Macys. I don't realize I have one black flower in my earlobe and the other earlobe is bare upstairs in the special room at Strand Books, listening to several brilliant readings by poets and writers. A writer, whose name I can't remember, reads from her novel maybe set during medieval times, about a dwarf child and how the parents tie the boy to some sort of contraption to stretch the child forcing him to become a normal height, this terrifying torture, which of course is pointless. As a short-in-height person, the scene sticks in my mind, actually it scares the shit out of me. I feel horror and nausea and I wonder if there should be a limit on subject matter such as child torture at readings? I find the earring on the floor outside the elevator. The earing has survived because it is of no value.

On my way uptown, the process of the journey, this great advancement trotting along 14th Street, a disheveled street I dislike, to catch the A train, makes me think of how much civilization has improved, that nobody would ever consider physically stretching a child in 2021, so why go back to dreadful moments, well, I guess the answer is to acknowledge the world gets better and better in comparison to what it once was, but not everywhere at the same time. Things happen in stages. My heart fills with such elation, I want to live forever to see how everything turns out for the human race.

The express train takes me to the 86th Street stop. I walk down to 82nd Street, which is a lovely quiet street and in the shadow of a huge tree I see a man pissing. He is well-dressed and unsteady on his feet, but that doesn't make it right. Further along, sitting in the low lights and glimmering charm of a typical New York bistro, where my friend is waiting to kiss me on both cheeks, to lift the weight of the world from my mind, to clink wine glasses and say, salute, this night of my life in the magic and warmth of friendship with my dearest friends Viviane, Gerald, Daniele and Nikos.

The urban concept of Manhattan embraces the human tides shopping all day, skateboarding along wide sidewalks of hurry and salt. With my overflowing shopping bag, immersing my fake self into this ballet of the sidewalk, keep to the right, the 'you can make it here' well-dressed striding of New York on asphalt laid down in 1871 where the drunks with vacant expressions now wander in tremulous defeat. Sidewalks embody the drama of refinement versus barbarousness, a site of supremacy, defiance and endurance, the endless passing by, an accumulation of hesitations, intervals and the occasional mugging and many obstructions, mailboxes, trash cans, parking signs, household rubbish, street operators, hustlers, food vendors, demonstrators waving handbills and in the middle of the footpath, a person of indeterminate sex wearing a blue fake fur Statue of Liberty outfit, why it is fur I have no idea, maybe because it is winter. The statue stands legs astride and holds a placard and hollers,

We will do your taxes and tell you jokes.

Which is the last thing in the world I would want. Later, I see the statue holding the statue's head under one arm, this dejected figure, walking down Broadway. For some strange reason the costume has a long furry tail.

Give me a flood of external sensations too enormous and insignificant to grasp, making my mind as blank as the cracked pavement, taking me past the bundled and shivering, the store windows weeping with condensation, frowning men consumed with business, the empty cabs hugging the curbs. Look up at the stone buildings with protrusions of cherubs, lions, gargoyles and cornices. Give me a sign.

Two Labrador's trot past in purple rubber galoshes and following them, an urbanite French bulldog with a bully-for-me expression, wearing a snazzy sky-blue windcheater.
A poodle shakes each paw trying to rid itself of tiny leather boots. A homeless guy couldn't make it here, not well-dressed, asleep against a dustbin, five Uncle Toby's breakfast bars in his lap, gifts from a stranger this evidence of kindness.

Isn't achievement the fools' gold of idiots?

My favorite names are Rudolph, Griswold, Potter, Pinwither, Norman, Gus and Detective Sergeant Footloose.

Hullo quite a nice big cow on Broadway, a fake cow made of an indeterminate substance, possibly a bull, standing outside the butcher shop, that also sells burgers and beer.
Hamburgers are so big and popular here, but everyone already knows that.

The light changes for a dinner at Carmine's where an old woman with a disturbing cloud of hair like a rat's nest, the color of faded apricots, sitting alone, tackling a plate of meat balls the size of a planet. At another table, a tiny Japanese couple consume an enormous salad, two plates of pasta and a beef rib eye steak that could double as a murder weapon, not even a smidgeon of barbeque sauce staining their lips.

Customers lean in to hear the waiters sing,

Come on everybody happy birthday.

Happy birthday to the wrought iron chandeliers and ceiling fans turning above walls covered in framed portraits and what else. Eight or so waiters scurry past a flower centerpiece five feet high and just as wide. These waiters work fifty hours a week, they carry mountains of food piled on platters, held high, armed with a sense of urgency, darting about the restaurant, urging to pass the food around, family style and go on, drink as many four-liter bottles of wine as you want. Excess is love.

Light from the kitchen illuminates the busboy drying plates by hand, one plate per second to the sounds of crockery being stacked then the swing door swings shut. Imagine a wild river of clashes, clatters, crashes of knives, forks this huge kitchen frying, roasting, boiling churning behind those swing doors and the locals bolt down their food and ask for the check while we are still tucking in our napkins.

To the sound of smashed plates and waiter yells,

Preceding party.

As black mom and dad reach across the table to hold hands and say grace, for what we are about to receive may the Lord make us truly thankful.

but is it art?

What do major works of art have in common? Stubbornness. Survival. They've made it this far on a journey through the vagaries of history. Art, literature, music must survive what a human cannot. The test of time, that old eroding bugger, that battering ram, our enemy, murderous, disappearing time. The epochs, generations, seasons, minutes, hours, days, months, weeks, years, more weeks, more days, more centuries. A true work of art, in its own becoming, becomes timeless, proving itself by surviving the victorious endurance test of time. Imagine art as flames, some art works flicker as a lit candle, others burn out to a smolder, the best and strongest are a roaring fire warming the soul and burning mass culture to the ground.

On one stay in New York, I accompany artist and writer Roberta Allen to a few exhibition openings in Chelsea, where the dogs have purple fur, the wine disappears as fast as the light of a firefly and the art is messy, forgettable, fun and not that great.

The Morgan Library & Museum once belonged to the heavily mustached rich financier balding banker robber baron John Pierpont Morgan, who canceled his trip on the Titanic and was mistrusted by reformers and muckrakers.

The Morgan owns original correspondence tapped on a typewriter by don't kill that mockingbird author Harper Lee. She begins her letter with *Listen you fool...* And signs and dates the letter, New York, August 17, 1960 then mails it to Robert E Bell author of the novel, The Tree published in 1959. In her message, Harper Lee underlines the words, *insist, must* and *The Tree*. She admits to *an almost pathological shyness, laziness and general confusion, first brought on by starvation and now by eating everything I can get my hands on.* Familiar traits, yes female characteristics. Harper Lee's passionate tone gallops through the letter highlighted by such words as: *afflicted, hideous, hated, masterpiece, extreme, luxury, yelling, absolute, yanked, cocktailing, nuts, doldrums, utter dreariness.* The letter ends with: *I wish I could find words to tell you how much I love your work. Love, Nelle.*

In a small dark room, we find glass cabinets displaying ancient eastern cylinder seals. I whisper to my friend,

Try and recite ancient eastern cylinder seals ten times as fast as you can.

He is far too evolved to play word games. Each seal is stamped with a singular narrative, as if a micro story about nobody we are likely to know.

Male figure before a goddess drawing aside her mantle.

Leaping stag with tree on mountain.

Hosts before a shrine.

Tree with winged sun disk above archer attacking lion griffin.

Kilted hero attacking felines menacing horned animals.

Hero pursuing two ostriches.

Worshipper facing armed God standing on bull.

Two figures attacking bearded figure with curls.

Attendant waving palm whisk over table before seated King raising cup and attendant with fan and towel behind King.

Armed hero grasping a kicking ostrich.

Worshiper behind two fish men with pollen baskets.

Three stags with a plant.

Goddess astride bull-headed dragon and aiming star-studded bow at lion griffin.

Griffin demon tearing branch from a tree.

The griffin demon in a filthy rage after discovering the price for a cup of coffee is six dollars in the museum cafeteria. The Metropolitan Museum of Art takes a moment to reflect on my friend and the Countess resting aching feet where the whole world sits on the front steps, our secret rendezvous and later in a room moldering with unvisited loneliness, wearing my sealskin coat, a faint color stealing into my cheeks, loving the straight up- and-down streets of New York, the big honest labels on everything, thirsting for the marvelous art and faint implications. My friend says,

It's a great museum.

I make my friend stand face-to-face with the brass head of a gorilla, his doppelganger.

According to an art expert who is a nun, it takes seven full days to properly experience The Metropolitan Museum of Art. This wilderness, a gothic-revival beaux-arts neoclassical baroque palace constructed of Indiana limestone (chosen because it's cheaper than marble) decorated with baubles, festoons, fretwork, arches and tall Corinthian pillars, dull behind the garish streak of yellow taxicabs out front and ever-present stars and stripes flapping high on a flagpole. And when the light changes, The Met transforms from a pinkish-yellow to marble tones reflecting a weak winter sun giving the building a proud expression as if saying, I feel strong calm solid.

No, the Met.

I search the eight medieval galleries for Mary Magdalene's tooth. The year before, I saw this Reliquary enclosed in rock crystal stored in a gilded copper cage and I always wonder, how they actually know it is her actual real true tooth. Can some sort of DNA or chemical test be done to prove its authenticity? Does anyone ever know the why the how to prove something is real? How does her tooth come to be?

Here. In the Met. I don't believe it's really Mary Magdalen's tooth. Today I refuse to have faith. In anything. I don't believe the Met owns two million works of art. They must have lost Mary's tooth. I refuse to believe that the tooth is misplaced. I am feeling toothless even with teeth and still I can't find the tooth. But small things do go missing.

And now we are lost. It will take seven days to find the exit. I don't believe in the exit. And being lost in The Met is lovely, for time here means nothing among timeless paintings that mean everything to do with wisdom, questioning why do we get so lost in our own anonymity and invisibility? The word lost stitches our clothes together, it wanders alongside us, it falls onto a page that can no longer be found, the lost pages themselves fallen maybe into a utopian splendor, submissive to the magical, the colors, the composition of our surrounds as we head to the European Paintings and stop for a break in Gallery 634.

An elderly German tour group glide as one entity into Gallery 634. They all wear sensible khaki trousers, socks with orthopedic sandals and crisply pressed shirts. A white-haired woman bites her fingernails as they assemble in a tight semi-circle around a self-portrait of an aged Rembrandt. The tour guide wears a knee length tartan skirt and Mary Janes as if the job forbids looking sexy. The group leans forward and listens intently to the guide's spiel.

This portrait of Rembrandt, painted in 1660, the medium is oil on linen, one of many self-portraits he executed over the forty years of his lifetime. Scholars interpret Rembrandt's self-portraits as an attempt to create a visual diary or a storehouse of facial expressions. Note how the artist confronts the viewer directly. Note the rich range of pinks and flesh tones. Note how the light effectively highlights the left side of his face and hair.

Rembrandt glares at the tour group. I look at Rembrandt raising his eyebrows, drawing his eyebrows together, the deep furrows in his brow. Rembrandt's expression gauges his mental state. Those perturbed lips, a shock of wiry gray hair bunches under a large black velvet beret. Yet note the stylish, jaunty, devil-may-care upturned collar, the oversized hat revealing an indulgent nature, the hat a fashion of the time. Rembrandt's possible mood of quizzical impatience, a little disconcerted, fussily piqued, combined with a touch of nonplussed innocence. Rembrandt with an air of slight annoyance, huffing,

I am simply not enjoying the rubbernecking anymore. I'm over it.

And with growing irritation asking,

How did I get here? Is it time for luncheon yet? Why are you all staring at me? Go away. Leave me in peace.

A man sits on the bench beside me. He gestures. All natural proportions. It's genius.

Yes, I reply, Genius.

Careful what you say, the self-conscious Rembrandt still looks worried. Is he fretting about his hat?

Do you think this hat suits me? Or does it seem too big for me?

The reverential tour group tiptoes away, hands behind their backs, soft whispers *don't touch anything* fading with them disappearing into the next gallery, much to Rembrandt's obvious relief.

My friend and I retire to the splendor of the classical treasures in the Greek and Roman Sculpture Court, the grace and virtuosity, the restored chariot, the dramatic drapery, male and female entwined, honed muscles, supermen and the levels of meaning for those who created them, those who discovered and purchased them and in the museum those like us standing before their magnificence. This enduring immortality of the sensuality, the drama, the violence of these elaborate masterpieces. But for the mutilations, not one bust or statue has a nose intact.

What does it feel like to be in bits? Do you suffer defeat or the gloriousness of victory? This death in battle, this lording it up, this handsome general, the hidden lives, the dead lying in unvisited tombs, the solemn expressions, no laughter, the perfect buttocks of the Three Graces, women objectified. The marble sculptures smack of wars and killing and ancient civilizations. I imagine them steaming up mirrors, thrusting swords into the liver of an enemy and charging off to orgies. I wonder if they are bought or looted. And is there a special place for all the pieces of noses and arms and hands? No there isn't. Stop focusing on what is missing. Appreciate the real presence of what is here.

I am. Here.

Tough times. Roaming and pillaging and burning and that Roman head looks like one of the doormen at our apartment block. But without the razor stubble.

We are walking through Central Park in the snow of a thousand years. On our way to the Guggenheim, we meet the Venus of Willendorf, immortal symbol, flower of the gods, beautifully rare, superbly erotic snow woman with a smile made of twigs.

I put my arm around her shoulder, she is rounder than the globe and as frozen as the tip of my nose.

Take my picture. Hurry before she melts.

No matter what anyone says, the Guggenheim is a bonkers pudding bowl slippery slide and cruel to make us walk uphill, but I find delicacy there.

On his first visit to the spaceship Guggenheim, my friend pays sixty dollars for two tickets and ignoring the crowded lobby, we take the elevator to the fifth floor. Always begin at the end of an exhibition. We exit the elevator and stand astonished in the curved space of bare walls. A vacant Guggenheim. This hollow void. A vacuum. Blank walls inside a gallery. Waste of the space. An insult to all artists. And I feel drained and dry to the core like an overcooked biscuit, I feel as empty as the space, I feel like I will never pee again, I feel sagging and airless and dizzy and I want to kill someone. My friend suggests,

Take a look over the edge.

Not funny.

Vertigo worsens inside a spiral space. I flatten myself against a cavity. Our devastation remains sedate and intact like a contraceptive device as we walk down the ramp of the glaring rotunda. The bare walls seem to mock us. There's nothing here but our stupidity. We are alone here with questions.

Do you think that's the exhibition? Nothing?

It can't be, there is no one here.

Do you think that's the concept?

No. Maybe. Of course not.

We reach the vast ground level and notice two young students dressed in jeans and black T-shirts, writhing together as they lie on the floor.

Well I think, that's kind of rude. Making love in a public space.

Nobody stops them. Are they dancers? The actual artwork? A piece of art not of stone or marble, but flesh and bone. A concept capable of looking back at us. The continuous flow of movement, drawing attention to human relationships. Ephemeral and short-lived, like my attention span. I understand the meaning, but I am bored senseless by the performance.

The boy and girl assume several positions. Sitting facing each other, lying on top of each other or underneath, sideways, spooning, his hands on her shoulders, slow movements, languid, vaguely erotic, like horizontal ballet. The young man, his red hair a distraction, flings his arm out, curves a hapless gesture, an embrace, then plays dead. The girl straddles him, her legs apart, toes pointed. Ah Rodin's sculpture The Kiss. Poses referencing erotic works from Courbet to Koons. Still boring.

A row of ten weary people sit on the ledge surrounding the indoor pond. A nursery rhyme pops into my head, *ten green bottles hanging on the wall and if one green bottle should accidentally fall...* Is that art? Four spectators remain on the ledge. I start humming, *four green bottles hanging on a wall...* A woman stands up and strides towards the exit. He asks,

Is that all there is?

You forgot to add 'to life.'

And me the petulant, ignorant, childish grumbling woman grumbles,

Do you think they are simulating a kind of choreographed sexual intercourse? All this half-hearted rolling around seems a bit grubby. Stupid Guggenheim. Sixty bucks! Bloody awful idiot spaceship building. Let's ask for a refund.

He rolls his eyes in the direction of a small figure.

Is she part of the show?

The square figure of a lone Japanese girl stands two feet from the contorting couple. This girl, dressed in a furry hooded puffy jacket, woolen skirt, white boots and her expression as blank as the walls. Her head tilts to one side. A voyeur with piercing eyes, this last remaining observer does not move, deep in concentration, the Japanese girl stares and stares. The couple glance up making sure they don't bump into her as they roll around. The Japanese girl takes a tiny step then another tiny step, inching closer and closer. Exposing this interloper to conceptualist art. Is she torn like us? Asking herself, should she stay or flee? Oh the young with oodles of time to dwell, to feel disquieting compulsions, to be fascinated, not jaded like me, not over it, like me. Does the Japanese girl know anything and everything becomes art simply because the artist says it is art? Does she question risky artistic ideas? The fact of the exhibition today at the Guggenheim, a work of art capable of leaving without a trace. The purity of absence. Will the Japanese girl ask herself the unforgettable persistent question? Is it good art? Does she understand the statement the artist makes? In a world overloaded with objects why create yet another bit of flotsam? Does she realize the action is for sale, the price tag, seventy thousand dollars? The Japanese girl does not demand an explanation or a catalogue, labels, prices and mementos. But I do. I need junk from the museum shop to feel part of what I see. Should the Japanese girl be a regular participant in this rolling around apparently named, The Kiss? I picture two copulating mice and a cat, the Japanese girl in the role of a predator, ready to pounce.

That day, the museum deprives us of visual splendor. The museum fails us. The museum robs us. The museum, not the art, provokes me and I realize the art, well it's supposed to provoke, to activate, to inflame the brain, but I remain as empty as the echoing space. This ability of art to disenchant.

Disenchantment makes me tired and fills me with world-weary art-weary dissatisfaction being too impatient to watch time fritter away, refuses the arousal of my curiosity for I don't need to be told the human body can be a work of art. I know this and the idea of being told makes me cranky. This quiet hopeless rage remembers the uplifting and enriching David Smith retrospective in 2006. His drawings in space, the welded lines figurative, landscape, abstract, ignoring the significance of the vital mass. These hollow places at the heart of his works filling my heart to the brim with the spiritual. I remember the drawings by Cy Twombly at Dia Beacon, the heart stopping scale, the beauty of his marks on paper.

And then I pause in defeat, for there is no point in comparing, no use in ranting and complaining, for that creates such a misuse of energy, a desecration of time. It does not rouse me from my complacency. I do not appreciate a space devoid of objects. I do not delight in the scuffs and smudges on curved white walls. My thoughts will not linger on this fleeting performance. The memory of it will evaporate the minute I pass through the automatic doors. The museum starves me as a consumerist, itching for tangibility, for temples of objects, for the transformed medium. Craving the sensibility of materials, the paint, the graphite, the bronze, the marble, the canvas, the paper and the frames that say, beautiful.

I am consumed with a sudden longing for the Met, for MoMA, for Rembrandt's rubble features, yearning for the enchantment of Music-Making Angels, hungry for The Spanish Singer, The Funeral, The Brioche, The Starry Night, for The Potato Eaters, Composition II in Red and Blue, The Red Studio, The Blue Window, The Large Nude. At least make it a requirement that the two performers at The Guggenheim be nude, make it real sex, for it's a fact that nakedness always draws a crowd of experts wearing elegant black and pontificating, but is it art?

We consult the New York Gallery Guide and walk along 18th Street in Chelsea, our destination the Meatpacking District, the goal, a favorite occupation, to view the countless contemporary art galleries, co-operatives, non-profit, sculptural, site specific, minimal, realist, ethnic, ceramic, figurative, political, conceptual, cutting edge, African American, emerging, North American Indian, Latin American art and the mothership gallery of them all the Gagosian, a gallery that the art critic Jed Perl described as what money is doing to art, or how the art world lost its mind.

At this point I must mention an artwork named The Literature Sausage made of minced books, texts and words mixed with fat, gelatin, water and spices then stuffed into a sausage casing. Really this is love.

We wander through the immaculate white voids of lofty gallery spaces, a desk in one corner where gallery employees hide behind a high partition, just the top of their heads visible, quite unfriendly, segregating themselves to avoid the ambush of ambitious artists, the Greenwich Villagers, Manhattan's children, a ricocheting bullet, midgets, big shots, the cashed up Upper East-siders, the perverts, the gangsters, the art lovers, the Gophers from Hell's Kitchen, the therapized elite, cops and the oohs and ahhs of the unwashed snickering, coulda done that with me eyes closed.

In an artist's co-operative, we find a series of tiny cubes constructed from resin and bone dust. We find air vents made from red velvet and satin ribbons. Deeper inside the space, we find the marks of a hundred buttocks left on a bench seat and for an appropriate finale, we watch a video of a blue synthetic elephant being pounded with a polystyrene tray of roasted mushrooms. I think of how painless that must be, of the absence of smell, yet the reek of ridicule, the wordless piece, the lyricism of a blue elephant with milk-laden breath and I understand that roast mushrooms must shrivel in the cooking of them, but these are plump mushrooms without the strength to kill.

We move on to a gallery on 20th Street and stand before a drinks cabinet in the shape of a gorilla, the primate's chest flapping open to reveal a gold-leaf interior with a plastic table and of course an algae-colored lump of felt growing out of the floor. Where is the roar, the chest thumping? Where is the bombast, the wisdom, the vigor, the whiskey? Where is the personal, the perceived? This bogged down piece by an artist working in terrible silence, drunk with dreams. Why not exhibit a pile of potatoes, a thousand sets of dentures, the contents of his medicine cabinet or just dust and empty words? There is always plenty of filth and meaninglessness. And the addition of a phallus of felt, such nerve, such tastelessness or maybe whimsy. Someone will buy it and their astonished acquaintances will gush and encourage them to go and find more artwork of equal hideousness.

He says,

You're being too harsh.

Bollocks.

My favorite piece is two ceramic tables brimming with bone-colored porcelain limbs, skulls and piles of sagging breasts and around the table some chairs constructed from guns, a perfect gift for the man who has everything.

I think it's mandatory for all things and thoughts to be life-size or bigger. Eliminate the inconsequential, the common objects and let us stuff our houses with the kind of art that brings on a seizure, causes a liver to fail, the heart to palpitate and make a normal person go berserk.

We both discuss the improbability of hundreds of quills inserted into an ornate helmet resembling a porcupine. The actual helmet claims to be an ordained helmet, which means the quills act as prayer antennae and receive signals from God. I look out the window to the heavens and hear, not a voice from above, but sirens. The atmosphere crackles with the distinct nonappearance of God. Never mix art and religion because it's kind of an irksome thing to do.

Next a surprising work, we come across a soaring installation of a taxidermy tower. At the top is a peafowl on top of an eagle on top of a lion on top of a cow. Thank god for the dearth of porcupines and gorillas. These stuffed animals gaze down at a high circular base that the cow stands on and around the outside of the base is a sculptural clutch of bronzed musicians with trumpets, violins, their mouths open wide in a silent scream. I identify with the silent scream.

In a moment of nostalgia, he scratches his head.

Ah the insanity of history and art cobbled together.

What, you mean the massacres, suffering, persecution and taxidermy?

Etched on his baffled expression, makes perfect sense of my reason for living, this and all absurdity becomes mine, loosening my spirit, giving meaning to my departures from reality, of using ludicrous images to achieve wordiness and the coincidence that this nonsensical accident of life here on which I perch on top of the peafowl on top of an eagle, on top of a cow, my friend on top of the lion. We are not bronzed, we are not screaming, we are not sweating, at least I am not. We are walkers on the wire, we are holding our breath, we are stubbing our toes, we are tipping the waiters, we are savages shaping our consciousness by looking at art in a fever, in the flesh and in the innermost doing, feeling, bumbling along hand-in-hand, we are moving closer to each other.

On Wednesday evening, we dress in our best black clobber and attend the opening of a live performance called Risky Business by an acclaimed Finnish performance artist, held in a gallery describing itself as 'a fearless little non-profit space in the heart of the Chelsea art district'.

The gallery is crowded with groups of students dressed in uniform black, congealing in a cloud of hangovers and cashmere-clad art intelligentsia with freshly gelled hair hovering in front of a rickety card table.

The artist, his head freshly shaved, wears a tuxedo, black tie and a stoic expression. He begins with never-ending patience, to carefully unpack twelve boxes of champagne flutes, which takes a wretched long time and results in us drinking more wine at five dollars a glass. After the glasses are unpacked, the artist proceeds to stack them in a snug formation, right-side-up and upside-down on the card table as if he is a waiter preparing a champagne fountain at a cocktail party. He places a second and third layer of flutes on the first layer and fills each glass with champagne. And even more excruciating, a recording of a male voice recites a hypnotic litany of arbitrary yet familiar words and phrases. The names of big corporations, world leaders, PR slang, slogans and military jargon drones through speakers located at both ends of the room. *Big Bang, genesis, creation of world, luminescence, spirit, soul, matter, angels, Hell's Angels, bureaucracy, ambiguity, counterculture, faceless, news, blackout, agent orange.* My friend creeps over to the bar and buys two more glasses of wine. I stare at the floor and decide I hate concrete.

The artist then kneels down on the floor and crawls under the card table. To create more space, several people flatten themselves against the gallery wall. Everyone is thin so that helps and the artist maintains a poised no-nonsense sincerity. Somehow he balances the table on his back and creeps on all fours, steadily inch-by-inch across the gallery towards a blank wall. The table wobbles and a few of the glasses fall smashing on the cement floor. His journey crunching through shards of broken glass, across the gallery floor takes an excruciating fifty minutes. I can only think of kneepads. He reaches the wall after leaving a trail of shattered glass and wasted champagne. Then the artist struggles to his feet. I can only think of my aching feet. The artist stands beside the table and bows. There is nothing I can do but stand there and wonder who has to clean up the mess he made in this fearless little non-profit space? Do we applaud? Are his knees bleeding?

I am a Philistine dying for a drink, eyeing the foaming floor and remembering that Goliath was a Philistine and I am furious at the artist who seems unapologetic for this shameful squandering of champagne.

Yes it's risky business crawling through shattered glass, dealing with my hostility, my indifference, my ignorance, my female preference for a clean floor and if you break something or spill something you're in trouble if you don't clean it up. And tell me, where is the beauty? But for the champagne.

patience and fortitude

Have you seen my buttery textures, the curlicues and happy gargoyles? Have you seen my two companions? Patience and Fortitude, the two marble lions guarding The New York Public Library. Patience and fortitude essential to survive The Great Depression, to overcome sadness, hopelessness, every problem, you are not the only one, this library has lions and from high to lofty, every allegorical statue of literary value, of history, romance, poetry, religion, drama and philosophy follows me into the lobby of The New York Public Library. Every allegorical statue of literary value stands in awe beside me marveling at the marble veining of this classical palace and my friend and I ascend the stairs to the rotunda, the ceiling vault reminiscent of Florence, cherubs reaching for the clouds and asking,

Do you think we've overdone it?

With a mural depicting the history of the written word, beginning of course with Moses and leading us all the way to the inventor of the Linotype machine. I walk airily into the catalogue room and approve the vital spark of Renaissance oak desks and before going into The Rose Reading Room, I read a quote by John Milton above the door, *a good book is the precious lifeblood of a master spirit, embalmed and treasured up on purpose to life beyond life.* I think so too, the meaning there in the words, the essence of a great mind, a great book outlives the author by many centuries. I hear music, the hush intimidating me, I will live longer for being inside this majestic room, the golden room, the burnished room shhhh, this room for scholars, their pondering paints a morning sky on the ceilings.

I sit down at a long desk and point my toes inward, not daring to take a book from the shelves. My friend photographs me. I have an inelegant beret on my head and a stupid smile on my face.

In the library souvenir shop I buy a ring made of a plastic scrabble letter J. Also a copy of E.B. White's 1949 essay, Here Is New York.

Here In New York, there are endless chances of rejuvenation, with hot dogs and popcorn from street vendors, with raw glittering light, the smell of roasting coffee. As temporary settlers, we absorb the unknown grandeur.

This city now planting its streets with daffodils, tulips and hyacinths.

A small island of compressed poetry.

Some days, the pretty haphazard of too hot, too cold, siren sounds filling the apartment.

Ignore the Statue of Liberty.

The street trembles as a train roars through the subway.

A museum of the self, the exhibition is described as refreshing and thought-provoking. And no trigger warnings. Is The Body Exhibition a tactless and degrading violation of human rights? The preserved faces appear to be Asian. The unclaimed corpses mostly young men, donated by the Chinese government and it is rumored the cadavers are really Chinese prisoners that have been executed.

After seeing the polluted lung of a chain smoker, a jar full of fetuses, the set of teeth growing inside a womb, skinless corpses in poses of running, dancing, playing ball, having fun, do we require that many veins, the heart behind glass is more than complex, so much could go wrong. Is that an embalmed Chinese revolutionary sliced vertically in half?

We emerge flabbergasted and nauseous. At the exit, we notice a large Perspex box filled with hundreds of discarded cigarette packets. The terror. Even though we don't smoke. Remembering the yellow fat sticking to those female skeletons makes me straighten my spine and suck in my tummy, the dead and death prominent in my thoughts, one day we'll be dead and running skinless through meadows asking ourselves, do the dead shoplift?

The plastic dead of us says,

That was worse than the Catacombs.

Yes, seriously disturbing.

It's going to happen. To us.

I don't need reminding.

Let's find a bar. How about The Dead Poet?

And the night shall be filled with music, and the cares that infest the day, shall fold their tents like the Nomad, and silently steal away. Henry Wadsworth Longfellow

I need a Bloody Mary.

A Bloody Mary won't make you live longer.

But it will help.

shopping

And another day, shopping in the depths of an uptown store, Anthology, a stylish store selling clothes, knickknacks, BoHo jewelry, soaps, candles, extravagance I cannot afford. At the sight of a uniformed police officer, I say to my friend,

Wow even the police shop here.

The policewoman is in the process of escorting a girl out the door. My friend whispers,

That policewoman is not shopping. She's arresting a shoplifter.

In a large department store that shall remain nameless, I browse for three frustrating hours and buy nothing. Riding the escalator up and down and walking round and round looking for presents and finishing where I start. I pick up a small, elegant bag and hook it over my wrist, to buy or not to buy, that is the question. Why are there always heavy metallic chains attached to most American handbags? Every woman needs to carry chains or be chained in some way. My body aches. My head throbs. I love shopping. I hate shopping. My mush mind tells me to go home. Escape this department store, the lights, the airlessness, the crowd, but I can't find the exit. I complete another circuit, trundling like a weary beast of burden, finally locate the exit and as I push the revolving door, an alarm goes off. A burly security guard motions to a young girl beside me. She looks terrified. I suppose she is a shoplifter. I keep going through the automatic doors and cross the road and go down the subway steps and reach into my pocket for the Metro Card and freeze.

Oh Christ.

The small elegant bag hangs from my wrist. Not paid for. From a distance a siren sounds. I begin to shake and decide to go on the lam, too afraid to go back to the store and hand myself in, imagining myself handcuffed, a chubby Irish officer shoving me into a police van and from a jail cell, my one miserable tearful desperate phone call to him.

talk the tawk

Beefsteakandtatersvegetabesnumbertwenty –
injinhardandsparrowgrassnumbersixteed!
Waiter! Waiter! W-A-Y-T-E-R comingsir readnminitsir dreklysir
– twonsixpence, biledamand cabbage shillin, ricepudn
sixpnce, eighteenpence –at the barf you please –
lobstauceensammingnumberfour –yes sir!
George C. Foster

The voices of Manhattan sound vigorous and varied to me overhearing strange conversations in bars, on the subway, on the streets, funny cracks, these snippets of dialogue, the street-cries, the drifts, whines and lives come alive in my mind from just a few words, unimportant, sometimes poetic, sometimes accusing, stupid, vaporous buttonholes slipping past me and fading.

Where is the roof?
We are on it now.
I see the sky hasn't come out yet.

This joint's all right to get tight with a couple of friends.

You're darn tootin, it's a knockover kid, we're sittin' pretty.

Do you possess a .38 cartridge?
Dat what you shooting?

This town is a leech. Give me the pure air and wide-open heart of California, I'd go back there tomorrow if I could.

Honey, it's really odd, honey I'm telling you the truth.

You married a fucken whore.

Just contemporary gospel punk rapturous wankers.

Your squeaky bubble-gum secrets are safe with me.

Care for some tapioca pudding?

My tongue piercings are absorbing the cold.

We went back and forth all night on the ferry.

Read the instructions.

Oh why can't just us two stay here?

Do you have an itchy ear?

What's he bawling about?

How could I have lost my head completely?

We tie him to an armchair, we light matches and put them under his feet. He don't feel a thing, no sir, not nothing.

Still throwing stones?

Come here Caesar, here boy, you'll soon get used to the smell.

How on earth did he come to be lying dead wrapped in a United States flag and holding a firecracker beside a boombox playing The Star-Spangled Banner? Just tell me how.

Don't you dare ask me that. No friend of mine would ever say a thing like that.

I don't care for cocktails.

I'll send Willy around, that is, if he's not drunk.

Just throw in a twenty dollar bill.

I got nuthin at a bargain but a big piece of swamp.

There is something so sad about a person going to bed alone.

Isn't that dangerous?

I never saw a man drink so much liquor. It ain't human.

I am in a serene state now, as serene as I can ever expect to be.

Yo Bunny! What news from New York?
It's bloated with a glut of young farts, with cockroaches and Bundt cake and the frayed nerves of retired gangsters.
So we are no longer important.
You betcha. And as usual in New York, everything is torn down.

This is gonna stunt me for life.

Hell, that's no way to treat a woman.

Come in on the second refrain, not the first, now do it over.

Where did they put you this time? The drunk ward or the nut house?

Bloody Campbell soup can.
Well, it's the same color as blood.
What?
Tomato soup.
No it isn't, it's a much lighter red than blood.

Looky looky here comes my cookie.

There is only one star left.

I didn't do a thing in town except bite my nails.

If I only guessed.

I bet it's him what's poisoning the pigeons.

Why do you refuse?
I would prefer not to.
Will you not speak? Answer?
I prefer not to.

When do you consider a person intoxicated?

Aw, man can't yo take a joke?

It's worse than I expected, I mean first the search lights and the lies and the priest managing to fall into the fountain. I mean, what the fuck anyway? Oh you'll soon get used to the stink.

What's the matter?
I am suffering. I let the pudding catch fire.

Those cheap garlands debase what I truly feel.
Which is?
Mad about the boy.

Yeah I never beat nobody.

You got any money?

The judge give him ninety days.

Try prunes.
Really? Are you serious?

What does he do for a living?
He's a bootlegger.
I can't even imagine what that involves.

He's a bandleader. He stages fights. He's cocky and rich. He's a luminary of sorts, a debonair mystic. He is New York itself. It's all in his obituary.

Ah do declare Manhattan, ain't it just the finest city you ever saw? You betcha New York is the fairest of cities, it rises from the water, like you ever bin to Venice? Glorious just wholly glorious.

There is no use talking to you.

Why so glum?
My friend threw himself under a train at Times Square Station.

Right off the bat this stuff is gonna fill you with gumption, eat enough of it and y'all turn into a rooster.

Ah, humanity.

I can't stand a woman that refuses to co-operate.

Day I is born I wished they'd dropped me in the Hudson.

I sometimes impersonate a clam.

Put a red rose in your cleavage, do not fail, dearest.

I'd like to know what you are doing and where you are going. What pleasures are you pursuing?

Do think it's safe?
Peyote? Yeah. Your gonna see the stuff of radiance. You gonna feel glorious Gloria.

Moments of terror are good for the liver.

It's getting chilly my love. Let's buy a bunch of yellow tulips to light the way home.

I hear she ripped up her husband's Klan robe and made a few aprons out of it.

I heard it in the news bout the woman skewered by a vestigial lightening rod.

But how in God's name did she get up there?

He's gone down the Village in his plaid poncho banging his steel drum god he's a flatulent arse hole, good times eh.

I tipped him two quarters. I mean he did have to stop the taxi and urinate.

He will know nothing of the matter until it is too late for him to kill you.

Well that sets my mind at rest.

I beat him without mercy. He never whines when I cane him.

That chorus girl she got a heart as big as an iceberg.
Have you ever seen one?
An iceberg?
No, a heart.

Hey you musta got Jesus confused with Superman.

When I go, this place goes with me.

Go on.

It sort of breaks the illusion, don't you think?

I'm so pleased you are being honest. Do you want me to bring my guitar over and sing under your window?

Fuck off Romeo.

The doorman shouts as his friend approaches,
There he is. My best buddy.
His friend beams.
How you doin' my man?

I just saw Jesus on the way to a fancy dress ball.

My thesis is documenting unpopular similarities, for example a sock and a penis.

Satan is amazed that mice walk on water.

I bin a cop for twenty- two years and I never seen nuthin like that.

I just got one foot in the bath when I heard the stairs creak.

A feeble man walks an Alsatian dog and yells into his cell phone,

Morty Morty can ya hear me? We'll have to rethink the neck biting.

Yeah man, big rotten stars falling outta heaven.

You is barking up the wrong fire escape brother.

I'll pull the rope and see what happens.

Hell no.

Yes, but it's not the kind you mean.

I think sir, he's a little looney.

Do me errands on a Saturday got no time for a fuck even.

Swing it, baby.

I'm not wearing any underwear. How about getting me one of those glazed donuts.

She dyed her hair a hideous red. God I laughed, even when she chased me all the way down Christopher Street threatening to shove a bread stick up my ass.

He's gone to the next world.

All the lice fell off that child in one go. Such a relief.

Nancy's a ball of fire but her chicken soup is too watery.

Last night? I went to Mars, baby.

Just eat the fucking squash casserole.

God that's woeful mac and cheese.

I'm no drunken sinner, I gotta right to let loose a hymn from time to time.

How do you like New York?

Yes we moved to the Bronx so much cheaper, but me hearing's going.

Good drink cost big money here,

There's nothing like it!

Two couples leap onto the A train. Retirees from Florida, jovial husbands and wives, old friends, the men appear married to each other and also the women, what friendship does. The men with a layer of fine golden hair covering well-developed tanned legs. They wear loud Hawaiian shirts. One of the men swivels his head and shouts,

Where's Ruth-Anne? The last thing I want to do is lose Ruth-Anne.

His wife points at a plump miserable woman squeezed in between a couple of annoyed looking teenagers.

She's right there Ron. Are ya blind?

Ron grins showing crooked yellow teeth.

Hey Ruth-Anne! Hug a tree why dontcha!

I hear Frida mashed a banana in a small bowl then tossed it into the trash and danced up the stairs to her husband's closet and with a pair of sharp scissors she shredded all of his suits. That's what she's like, so unpredictable and me unprepared, gone to seed.

You are such a good sport, how's your husband? Still belong to that vigilante group? Something to do with dog poop on the pavement wasn't it?

In front of me, in the wholefoods express queue, stands a man with drooping shoulders, a meek Jewish man, wearing a black Kippah.

His five or six-year old daughter sips on a cherry soda and in a whiny voice she harangues her father.

It's Friday, no it's Saturday today, yes it's Saturday, isn't it, no I think it's Friday yes it's Friday, no it's Saturday. Is it Saturday Daddy? Daddy are you listening? Is it Saturday or Friday? I think it's Friday. Is it Friday? But it could be Saturday. Daddy Daddy. What day is it today?

He bends down.

I honestly don't know now. Try to be quiet honey, you're confusing Daddy.

The child opens her mouth. Red soft drink dribbles down the front of her pink T-shirt. Daddy does not scold the child. This resignation of New York parents to their outspoken children. Children loving the sound of their own voices. The father speaks calmly,

Don't drool honey, try not to drool.

The one-sided discussion between two black women walking along Columbus Avenue.

Wanda. Waanndaaa pay attention to me. It ain't yer job. It's *you.* Don't ya see? It's *you* Wanda. Nobody likes *you.*

Wanda's friend flashes long fingernails painted the glossy white of highly polished automotive lacquer. I feel great sympathy for the unpopular Wanda burdened with such an honest friend. And I can't bring myself to look at poor Wanda, shuffling past with her head bowed, invisible, disliked by everyone. I hope she retaliates when she realizes it's not her, but everyone around her. It's not you Wanda, it's everybody else.

Further down Columbus, an elderly black man leans on a walking stick. He shakes his head in disagreement with his female companion.

Ahmmah nooo missus aahh got no equalizer.

At four o'clock on a Friday afternoon, an obese white couple charge along the congested Broadway sidewalk. The man all sirloins and haunches, has thick dark eyebrows above desperate eyes. His pock marked chin juts out like a plump grub. Wearing enormous sneakers, he lumbers in pursuit of his equally monolithic girlfriend. Both of them wear greyish oversized shorts and flapping cotton shirts, the same lard color as their pasty and anxious faces. Every part of the woman's body wobbles with rage trying to get away from him. He shouts,

Would ya calm down. I only slept with your sister twice and nobody knows.

Okay, I think. Now we *all* know.

On Eighth Avenue, a young woman totters in high heels past the pride of midtown, the firehouse, Engine 54 Ladder 4, Battalion 9. The open double doors reveal two large fire trucks parked side by side. She stops to admire the polished engines. Emblazoned across the windshield of one truck is a sign saying, Never Missed A Performance.

The woman shrieks at her boyfriend up ahead,

Scott *Scott* wait a minute. You could be a fireman!

He ignores her and keeps walking.

At an afternoon matinee starring Sigourney Weaver, before the curtain rises, I eavesdrop on the conversation between a couple of gay guys sitting in the row behind us.

I have friend in Wisconsin, he's dating my cousin. He's much older than us. He's not taking phone calls. He doesn't have long. Yet I don't find myself with the need to jump on a plane and see him. I will keep just the memory of him joking, asleep and awake. Who knows what that means, maybe it's that time of life. His sister? Oh she died in 2001. Embrace the joy. She was very sweet.

After the final curtain, a woman so fat she has to balance on top of the seat, half turns her head towards her companion and asks,

What did you think of the play?

Well she was much better in this play than the last one. I can't even remember what it was called.

My friend and I attend a friend's art opening in Red Hook. A wizened woman turns to her equally wizened husband and discusses the substantial buffet of canapes.

Arthur what did you think of the food? I thought the food was good. Not the art. Did you try the salami?

He grunts,

No Dolly, I couldn't get near the salami what with fifteen women stabbing at it with toothpicks.

Outside Fairways Market, a skinny black man wearing a leopard skin toga trots past, unsteady in black patent high heels.

Who? *Who* is Norbert Bisky?

He pauses, putting one hand against a pole to avoid toppling over. He taps his foot impatiently.

Does anyone at that stupid agency know? How will I recognize him? What do you mean a red carnation? Fuck that.

Please don't ask him to leave. He'll come back and sit quietly, I know he will, no he isn't drunk, I don't know why he smashed the glass coffee table, it's not like him at all, yes all his dreams of literary fame are broken, but that's not why he went berserk, he's always so cool, I can't understand how he sneaked that hammer past the doorman, only a fool imagines he's in love, yes those are his cigarettes, if he doesn't return, let's go downtown to Hanks party.

Golly they do it big in this town.

doings in gotham

Columbus Circle. We watch an all-female Obama assembly. I join the throng of women. This is my first time at a political rally. A woman shouts slogans and promises from the podium. I listen to all the speeches that grow louder and more frenzied. The crowd cheers with great enthusiasm and so do I with gusto bordering on hysteria. After being exposed to ten minutes of political fervor, I am now firmly converted. My friend buys me a badge that says, Another Woman For Obama.

The apartment building fire alarm goes off and in a panic, he shouts,

We can't take the lift!

And he makes me run down seventeen flights of stairs. A huge fire truck is parked outside the apartment building. We watch five firemen drag a monster hose through the snow banks and slush into the lobby.The doorman tells us some wires fused and a dishwasher caught fire on level eight. We eye the size of hose and ask, How big is the fire?

A woman in her forties, skateboards along 94th street. Her pinched features make her face appear almost skinless like fine wrinkled cotton pressed on high cheekbones. Like the dead.

The woman's eyes slant from strain. She smiles with pleasure. Going as fast as she can, a corpse zipping by, one foot pawing the ground, faster faster, exhilaration heading towards Central Park.

On Lexington Avenue, I see such a strange sight I have to avert my eyes. An old white couple very thin and beautifully dressed in navy cashmere coats, silk scarves, a felt hat at an angle on the man's head. He has a gold tie pin. She wears nylons and a blue pleated skirt. Their appearance is immaculate, as if they are returning from afternoon tea at the aristocratic social setting on the seventh floor of Bergdorf Goodman's. They are both lying side by side on the filthy footpath, curbside. They are stiff and so still, his arm through hers. Their eyes are closed. They must be about ninety. I can't remember if he is with me that day. It's the kind of memory where the surroundings fade as I look for just a few seconds and don't have a clue what to do. Should I prod them to see if they are alive? Is it a performance? Has this couple chosen a busy street to lie down and die in public? For obvious reasons, I find this incredibly disturbing. I think someone is bending over them but mostly the pedestrians rush by ignoring them. Are they real? Aged mannequins flat on the ground, not in the middle of the footpath, but just on the curb, as if arranged in this particular position. Of course they are real. Or maybe they floated gently down from the sky or maybe they are waiting to be taken up to heaven. I don't know what happens next. I must have walked away without doing a thing. It's one of those moments that I need to relive, but as a different, kinder, more sensible person. We are visiting Ground Zero. The crowd moves slowly. Water flows into infinity. Names are carved into stone. Beside me a woman reaches out to the list of names. Her gloved hand points to the words, 'unborn child'.

On Tuesday, it's amateur night at The Apollo Theatre. We take our seats in the dress circle. He is bursting with excitement and me feeling whiter than white. On our left sit four generations of black women laden with sequins and heavy jewelry. We are invisible to them. On our right, two young white girls gulp beer from plastic beakers and gyrate half-heartedly. In front of a huge screen emblazoned with the Twitter logo, a DJ jumps up and down and screeches,

Blibbedy blah blip blip blah blah garble garble yeah! If yo'all ready for a song say yeah.

I already love it. Strong spotlights sweep over many vacant seats and the small audience stands up and shouts a perfunctory,

Yeeeaah.

The cry falls flat. The DJ replies with another stream of unintelligible words. He leaps and skips about the stage and shrieks,

I'm outta here.

The lights dim and within the dimming everyone hushes. A tiny Korean girl tiptoes onto the stage. Her long black hair reaches to her waist. She wears a demure powder blue frock and ballet flats. Under a fractured blue spotlight, she shimmies once, swiveling her small hips, a fleeting tap dance and then rooted to one spot, her left arm stiffly at her side and her right hand lifting the microphone to her lips, she opens her mouth and sings in a voice as deep as Ella Fitzgerald's,

Oh Baby...

The Harlem vacant lot contains the remains of an illusion, streets of honey-talk, where the heartbeat transforms into a drumbeat, the pink clouds of Sugar Hill, a clutter of subway kiosks, a blast of jazz music, the glittering hair of Malcom X, urban renewal bulldozing the slums, replacing them with apartment blocks cheerless as a prison, all god's chillun got wings, the hangers-on, the hustlers, the suckers song and dance night life of piano-plunking, tickling the ivories, ho de hi de ho Cab Calloway at The Cotton Club and big spenders, fourteen dollars for a pint of Chicken Cock whiskey and chitterlings, collard greens, stewed corn, fricassee chicken, streets just the same and houses like peas in a pod.

Tonight, Carmen, yes a night at the opera, the Metropolitan Opera House with its loud and tacky sixties interior, gilded scalloped ceiling, like dinner plates, the starburst chandeliers, gold-plated curtains, claustrophobic red carpet, red velvet, everywhere gold and red red red. What in the name of god were they thinking?

We sit at the end of row J. I hear the British accents of an older couple sitting beside me. The woman places her hand on her husband's right leg, the leg a few centimeters from my left thigh. This British leg twitches uncontrollably with weird muscle contractions. This is already becoming a distraction. What's wrong with the man. Excitement? Spasms? Cramps? Parkinson's? Calcium deficiency? Anxiety? Who can be anxious at the opera? Not the audience, here for the pleasure of sopranos, baritones, the costumes, the theatre scenes, the drama, the tragedy, oh Carmen, we love a rebellious bird that nobody can tame.

The orchestra begins tuning their instruments. Next to me, the man's leg keeps on jiggling. It comes, it goes, then it returns.

An agitated woman rushes down the aisle. Her red satin suit and red hat sprouting large red feathers seems quite normal here. For what other color but red would anyone wear to this opera theatre? The woman in red mutters over and over like the White Rabbit,

Oh dear I'm late. I'm so late.

She pauses beside our row. The man's leg jiggles harder. The feathers on the woman's hat go boing boing, every movement keeps time with the instruments tuning. The woman glares at us.

Excuse me sir, you are sitting in my seat.

We search our pockets for the tickets, which we show the woman, the ticket seating numbers corresponding with the numbers of our seats, so no we are not sitting in her seats, we are sitting in the correct seats. The woman gestures at the tight-lipped British couple. They shake their heads and refuse to show her their tickets. They refuse to say anything and they look as guilty as hell. The man's leg shakes even more furiously than before. *These rebellious birds that no one can tame.* The woman races back up the aisle and returns within seconds with a blushing usher. She points at the English couple and in a loud whisper accuses them of taking her seats. Then her voice rises a decibel and into an evil hiss,

Still they refuse to move.

Someone groans in the opposite row. *Nothing helps, neither threat nor prayer.* Embarrassed, my friend and I stand up and slide into the aisle. The British couple relinquish the stolen seats and shuffle past three people in the row behind us and wedge themselves into their assigned seats.

Such a small commotion. The squeezing, the shuffling, the red faces, the sounds of the orchestra tuning, the audience tittering, the pre-performance murmurs, the anticipation. Thank god the lights dim. The theatre darker now and we are happy to be less visible. With the feathers on her cap bob bobbing, the woman in red sits in her designated seat and removes her lively hat. The seat beside her is vacant. I imagine a calamity occurring to her absent friend making her late for the opera. The man's leg keeps jiggling behind me, less distracting now in its proper seat, but still really annoying and my friend begins jiggling *his* leg which I thump. I am not a nice person and I pretty much suck.

All of a sudden, it is silent...Ah, what is happening? More cries! It is the moment!

Another year, 2018 at an opera, walls still the color of hell, the curtain rises like a phantom to reveal a mass of blue light. The audience gasps as a diver swims down from the ceiling through blue and bubbles, projected images of the ocean. These aerial dancers acting as pearl fishers as if under water, haunting the soul, swimming slowly and gracefully. A hush descends. The tenor sings brilliance. We stare in wonder, we live as one, behold a goddess, she has come here among us, we fall to the ground, we sense delight and torment, destructive forces, forbidden love, this formulaic, corny soap opera narrative of The Pearl Fishers. A man in the audience leaps up and shouts,

Bravo!

I assure my friend,

It will only take a minute.

I promised Jess that I would buy her a certain brand of mineral make-up only sold at this particular cosmetic shop on Fifth Avenue. We enter a long and narrow brightly lit store with a small counter at the front and another larger one at the back. The assistant sits at the small counter. She appears bird-like and brittle, her bleached golden hair piled high in a French twist. Her age maybe mid to late sixties and she wears a white linen suit trimmed in gold brocade and a load of gold jewelry on her skinny wrists. Her arms are bandaged. A name tag pinned to her lapel reads, 'Gloria Goldberg' and she smiles showing unnaturally white teeth. She speaks with a pronounced nasal New York Jewish accent.

Can I help you honey?

This captivates my friend. I explain about the make-up. Gloria turns her head with great difficulty.

Oh yeah we do stock those products.

And she bellows to an old hunched guy at the back of the store.

Ira! Come and gimme me a hand.

Ira bobs up from the back counter. He seems reluctant to help. Gloria shoots us an agonized grin. She moves awkwardly, wincing as she reaches for the top shelf. Then eager to talk, she grabs a cane and limps to her chair.

You must excuse me, I had a car accident yesterday.

Oh God. Are you okay?

Oh no. I'm pretty bummed up.

She shakes slightly as she tells us her story. That one uh, over there...Ira can ya hear me?

And she points an accusing finger at the now sheepish Ira. With considerable difficulty and a tired sigh, Gloria continues.

Ira kinda dragged me down the street.

Ira looks at us and shrugs his shoulders. I interrupt her.

What do you mean 'dragged you down the street'?

Well that one...

We turn and stare at Ira.

Ira. Well he drops me off at the shop yesterday. As I gets out of the car, I closes the door and my coat catches in the door. Ira the stupid klutz starts driving away. Slowly at first. Ira's looking for the traffic and not watchin' me. He starts moving faster and faster. I run along beside the car screaming and screaming and banging on the window. He's a bit deaf and doesn't hear me. He speeds up.

Gloria looks resigned as if this happens to her every day.

Anyway as Ira gets goin' the car drags me. People on the sidewalk rush over and start bangin' on the bonnet of the car. Ira thinks they's trying to attack him or rob him, so he accelerates. Eventually a young man, such a brave soul, jumps right out in front of Ira and forces him to stop. An ambulance takes me to hospital for the night. Nothing broken, just a few bruises.

We murmur,

That's terrible. You poor thing. What a terrifying experience.

Both of us thinking, only yesterday and here she is back at work. Ira stays busy at the rear of the shop as if nothing has happened.

We gesture in his direction,

Your husband must feel awful about this. You should have taken a few days off.

Gloria grimaces.

Oh Ira ain't my husband. Ira owns the store. I bin working for that man for thirty years and he don't give a damn about what he did to me. Almost killed me.

Gloria hobbles to the counter and begins assembling the tiny boxes of mineral eye shadows, powder and mascara. Ira materializes and rings up the sale. My friend checks the receipt and says to Ira,

It's forty dollars over.

Can you please add it up again?

Nah dat machine's always right.

Don't think so matey.

My friend angrily picks up each of the products and calculates the correct amount. Ira scratches his head.

Dat computer must be playin' up.

Gloria leans heavily on her walking stick and rolls her eyes.

Whaddaya gonna do?

We are heading down to South Ferry to shuttle across to Staten Island. The train stops at Rector St and people get off and the train driver, speaking in a typical Bronx accent, announces over the public address system that when the train arrives at the South Ferry terminal only the first ten carriages can be alongside the station, so everybody in the last four carriages will have to exit the carriages right this minute and move forward to the first ten carriages. Apparently some people sitting in the last four carriages don't believe the announcement or cannot speak English or are deaf or don't want to hear or don't want to move or cannot understand what the train driver is saying. The train driver makes the announcement several times, but several passengers still remain in the last four carriages. The train driver must be able to see these passengers through some sort of video camera. He starts to get agitated, he starts raising his voice, he shouts,

The remaining passengers in the last four carriages please move forward to the first ten carriages. These are the only carriages from which you be able to depart at South Ferry.

It becomes clear that these passengers are still not moving. The train driver shouts even louder.

You people back there in those carriages you must move forward. Get out of those carriages.

He begins to howl,

The fucking train will not fucking move until you goddam passengers get out of those last four fucking carriages.

Eventually the train leaves Rector Street Station with the passengers in the first ten carriages sitting very quietly, very obediently and not reacting. I assume the passengers in the last four carriages are deaf, are still waiting for the end of the world or have been rounded up like a pack of sheep and bundled off to train behavior school.

We are down near Battery Point on the coldest day one degree or one degrees, when I see a man exiting a hotel lobby and all he is wearing are shorts and a T-shirt. I guess a business traveler, who failing to research the weather on his i-phone, has arrived in New York with only summer clothes to wear. The man shivers violently as he hails a cab to rush him to the nearest department store where he will buy a warm coat and have a rest from all that hypothermia.

On the ferry to Staten Island, its too cold to be on the observation deck, the sharp winds, the blustery scene, remembers a painting of a ferry ride to Jersey City, this rough crossing, the tilt of the frame, a listless figure, this painting is a second version after the artist quarreled with his wife and threw a chair at the first painting.

Look!

The light fog of a statue, her arm visible in a cream sky, the spiky crown and behind us the city, so we turn to look at the lights, rather than what is ahead.

briefly the burg

Brooklyn you know is much admired by the Gothamites. I know few towns which inspire me with so great disgust and contempt. It puts me often in mind of a city of silver-gingerbread. It has, it is true, some tolerable residences, but the majority throughout are several steps beyond preposterous. June 12th 1884
Edgar Allen Poe

I too lived, Brooklyn of ample hills was mine.
Walt Whitman

Brooklyn Ice-cream Factory, a stark clapboard building has windows trimmed in pale blue and a sign that says 'closed' which makes sense in the middle of winter.

In the heart of Brooklyn, we discover a tiny community museum, the City Reliquary, no admission fee, donation only for the viewing of forgotten collections. The place is filled with an overwhelming clutter of beer bottles, baseball memorabilia, subway tokens, this familiarity of peculiar treasures. And the delicate cursive writing, written on old sepia postcards, above a picture of some buildings in Manhattan.

Dear Pearl, Tell 'Velvet Eyes' this is where you expect to live when you get rich enough.

I pick up another postcard and turn it over. Clumsy writing surrounds an illustration of the majestic New York Life Building.

Dear Martha, This is one of those skyscraper buildings thirteen stories high. This building means look out for your life. Amen. Millie.

I imagine Martha and Millie as members of the church choir. Two slovenly yet puritanical women dressed in dowdy housecoats, Millie's hair up in rollers, a cigarette dangling from her thin lips, both of them gossipin' and rocking on porch rockers and beside them a butterscotch pecan pie cooling on the windowsill.

Martha criticizing,

You're nuthin but a flibbertygibbit Millie.

Martha probing,

Who dat man you seein'?

And Millie replying,

Thought I'd plant some doubting in that rapscallion's conceited mind.

Time fluxes, the storm clouds about to crash and he's asking,

What time is the opening? Six o'clock?

Yes. At this gallery on Flatbush Avenue Brooklyn. Homage to concrete floors and cheap merlot, the gallery's dirty walls lined with paintings of intricate webs like entrails painted with red wine on Belgian linen, skewing towards the dark shadows, the canvases seem to watch the hovering artist, a sinewy man-child like a black widow spider with long greasy dark hair, eyes outlined in Kohl, white wrinkles and small breasts. I want to tell him the facts. Wine is for drinking. Wine makes us as leisurely as a snail. Think of the silver snail trails. The randomness of where wine takes us. We are here for the free wine. Instead, I ask him,

Have you ever experimented with vinegar?

The spider cringes, his expression sour and insulted.

No. I *only* paint with wine. I am a cerebral artist. You must understand, the decipherability, the gossamer sensibility, the erosion of artistic freedom, the trauma, the transcendence for wine is alive, wine is life.

Oh right. I understand.

The heaviness of what goes unsaid. I am a slack-mouthed archangel. Words written on flesh. The skulls of tattoos. The stitched words. The bad spelling. The faint future. Wine fades. Cheers. Yes please, I'll have another. Another crushing. Another bore, more kitsch dancing to the hideous guitar music whining from a stereo on the floor littered with empty beer bottles and what appears to be mold. It's snowing in Brooklyn. Tired of the spider webs, I pick up a local newspaper. The death of art. The mosaic of murder. The collages of confusion. The paper features a few neighborhood crimes. Red Hook, man strangled. Cobble Hill, woman shot to death. Windsor Terrace, woman bludgeoned. Park Slope, boy stabbed.

My friend and I wander the streets of Williamsburg. I welcome the graffiti with an open heart, its dense layers all torn, scraped, ripped, then ripped again pasted over doors, walls, poles, trash cans and windows. Frenetic surfaces, almost unreadable, scratched posters and scrawled words and the occasional fluorescent twirl. Old patterns, urgent stickers, signatures, beliefs, advertisements, accusations word for word,

COST the pope of trash COST fat cat COST talk as dirty as you want and I will do the same COST COST FUCKED MADONNA soulful reveries COST let them do what they want to do it's not affecting my soul COST.

And painted on the side of a dark green trashcan, a horror movie scarlet inscription dripping paint runs down the side.

Nearby some tiny yellow letters.

The Worm Holes.

And stuck to a telegraph pole,

Red Dead Redemption.

Down the side of a red post box, a patchy list in italics,

Sulk ONLY and *Click Clack Boom.*

Some angry black spray paint commanding,

Kiss Elvis

On top of a scratched logo for Future Cop and underneath a cartoon block of Fools Gold, lots of hearts and where we can find *fascism top quality,* with a cartoon fist, the middle finger sticking up, *Fuck You.*

Taped over a mass of scribble, a white A4 sheet of paper announcing,

Tim's Tailor. We've moved upstairs.

This brief sane message covers part of the poetry, the graphic rage, the insanity, the love of *City Kitty I Love NY.*

Amen.

every girl's dream

The brass plaque screwed to the brick wall of No 13 Commerce Street Greenwich Village, a federal style house, says in uppercase type,

ON THIS SITE IN 1897 NOTHING HAPPENED

A star at the beginning and another at the end. My kind of house. This place of boo nada bumpkiss bupkis diddly-squat jack-shit jack-squat zilch zippo, nothing happens here.

But two doors down, something happened at No 11 Commerce Street. This is the house in which Washington Irving wrote The Legend of Sleepy Hollow.

First of all, enter the atmosphere of the Lower East Side, where its noisy, messy, rubbish, the glints, the dirt, the rush, all conglomerate as one organism rubbing and bumping and more elbowing me aside.

A bright red sign announces Dr Toothy's Dental Office. What an amazing coincidence. Has the name Toothy influenced a choice of career? My friend sighs and explains.

Dr Toothy is probably *not* the actual name of the dentist.

Knishes. They taste sweet. That's all I remember. The sweetness. Will you please call me sweetie pie in public?

Zig zag the streets, Orchard, Ludlow, Essex and on East Houston. Stop here.

And to the left or right, depending on which way we face, there is the arresting presence of Greenwich Village. The Village, being so far from Central Park, allows for a tighter landscape, outside the grid, quiet and civilized shreds of brooding, fundamentally elusive, of bohemian self-awareness, queertalk, hiptalk, hipper slickers, afternoons in bars, there is something in the air here, the Village vibe where pop poets migrate into clouds of smoke, the kooky word play, to die in taverns, listening to soulful grooves on nocturnal nights, listening to parties, for we are all searching for The Bitter End.

At Bonnie Slotnick's Cookbooks, a teddy bear waves from the store window. As soon as I enter the tiny shop, empty of customers, I turn around and leave. The smallness, the amount of books, there might have been frills, fake flowers, knick knacks and flim flammery (?) all so totally overwhelming and claustrophobic, anxiety eats me alive.

Bonnie Slotnick, a name exuding happy rhythms, clarity, conjuring a fairy godmother, a pastry chef, a charwoman, a calm and steady person who loves cookery books and ignores customers.

On red brick Bleecker Street the fire escapes climb up the sides of buildings like dinosaur backbones.

My friend bumps into a sprightly wrinkled chap outside Blaustein Paint and Hardware. This old queen of hearts, mad as a March hare, regales us with fluttering hands.

I need help. I just moved into my studio and in all the fluster, I locked myself out. All my possessions packed in boxes are dumped on the footpath. Street punks will steal my stuff and I don't have money for a locksmith. Do you have any cash? I'll pay you back.

A young bloke walking ahead turns and shakes his head. He mouths 'no' and makes slashing signs across his neck with his index finger.

We escape to a café, the tables set with plastic bottles labeled Drink Me, happy little cupcakes line up on the counter, the frosting spells out the words Eat Me. Which is oddly obvious. I think the chairs should say Sit Down. The salt and pepper shakers, Sprinkle Me. The sauce bottles, Squeeze Me. Doors often say Come In. The categorized universe of open, enter, exit, male, female, no entry, no smoking, slow down, private, welcome. A world created for people like me missing the entrance, driving into carparks through the exit and going up one-way streets the wrong way, even though a big red sign screams, Stop You Are Going The Wrong Way'. Sign sign everywhere a sign.

My friend chooses a chocolate brownie and buys me a vanilla cupcake, sprinkled with lavender petals. We sip the weak coffee.

He says,

Listen girl, throw pepper over your right shoulder, keep roses by your garden gate, eat lavender petals for good luck and fall in love.

My friend brushes the pale crumbs from my coat. He often calls me kid or girl.

Hey kid, remember the giant meringue you ordered in that café on Fifth Avenue? What an explosion.

Our little trip of falling in love with cheese blintzes, lunch at The Russian Tea Room, the trickle of rich red borscht on my shirt. Memories to keep in satin boxes, labeled valentines, columbines and crooked rhymes.

We finish the cake and still hungry, my friend reaches into his pocket and brings out a large red apple. He takes a bite. In this whole juicy world, he has an eye for apples. Big apples. Crunchy. Bitten right to the core which sounds sinister or deep as in drill down into every passing thought until the last crumb vanishes. I hum along to the song on the café stereo. *In a Bleecker Street cafe, I found someone to love today.*

One Sunday in March, its my birthday and our last weekend in New York. Good luck. Ice on the footpath. Still it's Sunday. The past goes away. A shorter future brings light and joy and tiny blossoms. Rub petals against my cheeks. See how they glow. A clear day sees forever and here.

My friend takes me to the Boathouse for an extravagant brunch of eggs benedict, smoked salmon, a table by the lake, crisp linen, silverware so shiny shiny, only in New York which begins and ends with shiny shiny. My friend reaches over and takes my hand.

Happy birthday.

Happy happy babe.

He hands me a small blue box.

I hear a long and splendid drum roll. Think of a soprano hitting the high notes. I hear glitter tickle. Every girls' dream. I imagine feminism burning me at the stake.

The city goes on without us. The city manifesto takes nothing from us, gives us everything, the Manhattan skyline rises from the Hudson, these traces of a New York life remain in fleeting reminisces, of Velvet Eyes, plastic pigs, Fool's Gold, tapestries, plummeting air conditioners, shoplifters, crossed teaspoons, the fog rolling in off the East River Bank, bagels, painted stares and best friends falling in love and yack yack yacking right through the very heart of it until the end.

prose notes

slam dunk

A sea change, a city change, change my nationality, become a native New Yorker and reject 'the normal' transforming into a different personification of normality, not as in abnormal, but not ordinary, being extraordinary, skedaddling along Madison in the M3 bus chiming nickels and dimes. Does this make me a traitor to my origins? No. Does this make me original? No.

What if luck commands me to be born in New York City and the contents of this evocative narrative (is it? maybe) suggests I live in a cold-water studio in the East Village and peddle stories to agents and editors telling me my work is fucking incomprehensible, so I slug a cop and run for it, this haste of dealing with the daily minutiae of grilling and whipping allows me the wonder of how can a person be?

You are so funny today New York, in a sense I am winning just by being alive, for having fun, for embracing the hours slipping by. What a day! The city grows wings, it's the little water tanks (is that what they are?) on the rooftops of apartment blocks. They don't seem to hold enough. Miracles. Love. Water. Remarkable derivations and stories happen on top of the many cupolas. Listen to me speaking the Italian language, *cupolas cupolas, hola!* No that is Spanish, that is foolish and eerie this immense falling of snow, but without hesitation, I soar on the wings of a city, beating my chest with surplus energy. The obvious result of excessive caffeine.

A military parade along Fifth Avenue after Trump is elected President leaves us all reeling and the memory of that show of heavy boots, camouflage suits ruining the day. New York, you are sad today remembering Mussolini shrieking obscenities, looking ahead at the years of embarrassments. Take heart in the fact you are a city of enlightenment, the subway rattling the pavements, children playing baseball in the parks oh the parks oh the parks, too much coffee again, this refrain and the bagpiper busker plays Amazing Grace at Grand Central where the skirl makes me cry for my Scottish ancestry, which gives me a horror of the suburbs, a cesspool of sameness, where wives blow their heads off with shotguns, but at least they escaped the sound of wrecking crews and sirens. And I am here learning the Rhumba, at a dinner party in a beautiful brownstone, but as usual the kitchen is small, and earlier that day, I see two homeless gypsy women, one is pregnant, camped out on Broadway outside Eighty Sixth Street subway and my friend Debra once tried to speak to them, asking if they need help and they were quite nasty even to strangers offering them food or those just rushing by on their way to the raffish congestion of downtown.

A greenhorn must gain an eclectic oeuvre by growing a new heartbeat, roots, a throbbing pulse and at night attend a Tennessee Williams festival held at a blues club. I must possess a distinct political vision and become motivated by the strenuous momentum of anticipation and enthusiasm. I must dress up in a bumblebee costume for Thanksgiving.
Why? Because of turkeys becoming extinct. I must

drink pumpkin ale and write an essay on grave-robbing. At Nathans on Coney Island, I must eat half a famous hotdog, this scum-pipe corndog bummer bite, which tastes terrible and now the annual all-you-can-eat-hotdog-eating competition for the underdogs and barking spiders and floosies who never sleep.

What does it take to discombobulate a city? Greed and ambition, stories of deception, ill-fated passion, ultimate forgiveness, the glorious score of Swan Lake, a performance with apple pie and baseball gloves and the Feelies onstage. Be true to myself, make a splash as a lanky lying freethinker or moonlight as a rambunctious cellist, banging on with so much anxiety over the cost of education, so I hide money offshore, rant about broken elections and go back to the nineteen sixties, become a whippersnapper flouting formal protocols and slamming reputable tastes, my brain like an exploding scrapbook.

I discover there is no such thing as a lady barber, that brunch is a fusion of lunch and breakfast and I am invited to blowouts, barbeques, block parties, shindigs, raves, meet-and-greets, *brunch*, yes, I shout, yessiree.

Some dumb shit dumb ass tells me his secret hidden in the glow of a streetlight hanging low under a lost moon, under a pile of candy-bar wrappers are paper packets not rappers. I might work as a coat checker at the Russian Tea Room. I might be as tightly wound as an art historian with a golden opportunity, hitting the razzle-dazzle notes. I carouse blithe and guileless at a sleazy off-Broadway opening night play on words for drunkenness, for stardom really turns stars into

assholes. I dream of Chopin's Marche Funebre Piano Sonata
this fight for life, always close to my heart.

When will I realize we are all talking about the same person?

The billionaires and the bigwigs, the connivers, the cheats,
the scammers refusing to reveal the tricks of the trade, slam
dunking a pimp with a manicure ooh dem cuticles lure a girl
onto the rare tenderloin where Fanny the lip hangs around the
Metropole and notices a variety of butter sculptures of cows at
a banquet, what about gluten anxiety?

In New York, decades ago, if I walked through the city I
might glimpse an illuminated white baby's coffin in the store
window of an undertakers.

It is dusk. I am not vigorous, but inventive in my attempts to
grapple with life's problematic obsessions and solo flights of
pretense in that I am pretending I live in New York City or
practicing to live in New York City, falling and cutting its face
on the ice somewhere near Washington Square, filling with
poets and students, this potential campus rife with influenza
and I ask why have all the banana-nut sundaes vanished?

The people of New York walk an average five miles a day. The
current swift of rush. The streets! The streets! My brain lights
up the map of no particular direction which translates as the
future *fifty years hence*. A passerby asks,

Can I give you directions?

Follow me, he says.

Just follow as I feel, just part of the living crowd, join the
living which is a vast improvement on the dead crowd.

My pervading order of architecture is Corinthian. I am stone covered with stucco, my breasts are white marble. I am a white CIS woman with iron beams of immense strength and solid walnut doors. I weigh over fifty thousand pounds and an extra thirty feet in depth allows my windows to be evenly spaced. From the sidewalk to the top of my dome is sixty feet, the dome appears heavy and cumbrous compared to the general characteristic of my structure, my upward sweep and ballsy robustness. I wish.

Is it wrong to be afraid of suspension bridges?

On the edge of Manhattan, the ebb-tide, the what, let me look ebb-tide in the face, the ebb and flow, how does the sea become a river? It just turns left. I am on the edge of Manhattan, some bluster, the water flows out, falls back to the sea pours into the Hudson River heading north to the Bronx. I am on the edge of Manhattan,waiting for the ferry to Dumbo, the beginning of a pale sun equals the dawning of feminism now drowning I suppose. I blame the feminists for the fact I have so much to do every day. Yet there is distance to cover to Dumbo which I love but would never name a child Dumbo. The flood-tide, the ebb-tide, the ebb and flow, the ebb refuses to flow, I would never name a child, Walt. I am on the edge of Manhattan together as one of the others, crossing from shore to shore with the gladness of the river and the bright flow. I would name a child Flo. I must feel when I look at the sea, is it sea or a river, they are both together, both confused below me standing yet hurrying to cross the river that might be the sea with its great lack of sails, haze, steamers, but wait I see ocean liners gusting those frolicsome crests impossible to miss, yes the ferry is here hurry.

In The Algonquin Hotel, I fall to my knees on these off-the- cuff-barbs and cutting remarks, a manifesto of dragging my private thoughts over the coals of self-satisfaction, ten pages laser printed at Brown & Co Stationers, the best place to pick up quirky postcards, tucked under my arm, my only qualifications, a deep appreciation for the consumption of alcohol, a talent for going around and around in vicious circles, without the ability to challenge the intelligentsia and the oppressions of the decade, just hungry in anticipation of lunch and vivid style, substantive views of contemporary society, biting wit, sparkling wordplay, hard-bitten sarcasm, significant jokes about the cultural landscape and enthralling commentary on social justice and personal freedoms, most of which I ignore because I simply do not have the time or energy to go out for lunch.

In the city, I am an alien here, the city is over there, the city is over me, I will never get over the city, but I cannot move closer. I am an alien to the city. I am an alien in the granites, the clay giants, the red white blue of this city, even on a dull day, or soft shine of winter sneaking sleet, the shock of icy wind that forces me to shelter in a doorway, the jostling tide, the blue masses, the slipshod south, the millions of artists, the brutal backdrops, yearning harmonies, the absence of rodeos and rain forests, the sound of fog horns long gone, the sputtering of awe and displaced desire. I am an alien Goth woman, combing my hair with a steel comb, a 'ready- made' by Duchamp and the liturgical comb made of ivory which is a terrible thing the murder of elephants, reminding me that a herd of elephants were used to test the strength of the Brooklyn Bridge, symbol of exaltation, where jobless men leap headlong into the Hudson. I am an alien here feeding on the

disappearing sky, the hilarious cold, I should visit Matisse, his exquisite frictions give aesthetic pleasure, this is my magic act, pull Liberty out of a hat, dancing alone in the sculpture garden in SoHo wishing for a flash mob,
discovering the combination of R&B and psychedelic rock is as combustible as planets colliding. I am an alien repeating myself and long running never ending scorching crescendos burning a hole in the soul makes repetition a good thing. Right?

What I find online that is indisputably New York urban culture and society which is puffy eyes, whispering it smells like pee, when I get on the subway, getting on an empty train seeing the homeless guy lying on a seat and getting straight off and dry retching, crying on the subway at 2 a.m., French bulldogs, black clothes head-to-toe, slamming New Jersey, vodka sodas, Flagels, Brooklyn drag queens, bumping into your ex at Marshalls, blaming your love life on Mercury retrograde, Lexapro jaw clenching, pathetically flirting with the super to get him to fix the broken locks, toilet and rodent situation, sleeping through my subway stop after Sunday brunch, improv classes with Upright Citizens Brigade, ordering a Trenta iced coffee at Starbucks, depression, Alec Baldwin at Ninety Second Street Y, complaining about the L train, street art that says, *don't forget to be awesome, kindness is free, pain is a good teacher,* Artichoke Pizza, avoiding the suburbs, throwing up on the Ikea ferry, general dislike for children, pretending to pray so that my Uber driver won't attempt small talk with me, Bushwick bangs, cheap tropical cocktails at Happy Fun Hideaway, random pathetic intellectual arguments, dismal shit coffee, dodging midtown, being poor, abstaining from dairy, robust immune systems, dogs in booties, ditching Chelsea for Harlem, broken umbrellas left on the sidewalk, anxiety, poking fun at vegetarians from Los Angeles, powerful calf muscles, a panic attack in the baby products aisle at Rite Aid, ordering wine on Swill, ten minutes later ordering a six ounce dark chocolate cookie from Insomnia Cookies and red velvet cupcakes from Goldbelly.

And I walk fifteen blocks with an ache in my lungs to buy an ice-cream at Morningside Park, no-one here, but for an addict selling a stinking leather case to a gimpy man. What's that smell?

Remembering George the Greek getting busted, what a goofball not enough moxie or too much, all too muchness, my eyes blasting like guns, you will not believe what I believe walking beside Whitman on the river streets of the courageous and friendly city of haste, just how he feels when he looks on the river and sky, so I feel, just as he stands and leans on the rail, this hurry and swift current. I stand yet to be hurried, with an inherent soul accepting the giant city's mayhem manic fervor as being natural and expected.

I believe lipstick is the work of the devil, that New York is constructed from the labor of individuals, that it's impossible for square steel and glass to warp in the presence of money and limited parking and the women of New York appear to be dehydrated streaks wearing fur coats and nylons, their eyelashes wet from snowflakes.

Here in the frantic haste of a metropolis, a bohemian finds amusing oddities of freak show quarrels, a dish of tender rosegoose, follows bilebeef and cabbage, a poet orders from The New Yorker. Th is poet, especially bad at writing novels, lives on Bleeker, with terrible digestion but in his view the belly must cope with what he eats, the lumps of butter so popular with idlers, firemen with the crackle of dollar bills deep in their pockets, ready to run at the first sign of smoke, ready to put their lives in peril to save a novelist who fell asleep burping and smoking in bed.

Now I am thinking about how egg shells here are pure white, the reason the whiter egg can be created is the color of the egg matches the color of the chicken's earlobe, so the chickens with the whitest earlobes are chosen to lay eggs in America but it's a fact, American eggs are banned in the UK because of the high risk of contracting a drastic illness from eating those white eggs, from chickens bred to lay white eggs, okay enough about eggs and whiteness.

I recall instead the man with the eyes of a trailblazer, he blows into town from the Corn Belt, gets caught up in the great tide of commuters, takes a bath in the blinding lights of Time Square at five pm its finest hour, such awesome light that rips at eyesight, tumbles, flips, zig zags, flashes and people drop like flies having seizures and the fog is useless as the glare fights with a searing spasmodic impatience attempting to send as many tourists to the point of insanity as possible and I hear the deadpan woman living to a hundred and crying,
    Oh lawdy dat sky is snooty and blunt and blue!

There is a murderous appetite within this hive of individual neighborhoods, observe the fear of decrepitude, how sewage drives away all the fish in the Hudson, this river once grew lobsters the size of Volkswagens, which I suppose is an urban myth. So remember the unfurling skyline at dawn, the suave thug-hunters and the high cost for a wheelchair pusher to take an invalid outdoors, the dog walker on the Upper West Side who strikes a pose when I take a photo, the young mothers with nannies pushing babies in pushchairs down genteel West End Avenue, quietly residential, are there storefronts here, no, the apartment buildings so quiet and unnamed as if anonymity lacks pretensions and also represents silence, calm on the eye, this beauty of buildings lavish creams, honeycomb exteriors and ironwork, except on one of my daily walks, I see ambulances and police surrounding a corner on Ninety Eighth I think, this apartment block where a man crouches on the roof anticipating his death, what they call here, a jumper, which is the name we have in Australia for a woolen sweater, where I think the name jumper has a correlation with sheep jumping, but I am lost now and I hurry away not wanting to see anyone jumping off a building. Where am I now in West End Avenue, a dream of pretty children with glamorous mothers dwarfed by ostentatious residences, well I am here with my feet on the ground and I'm turning left to walk back to tawdry Broadway, this unfunny rhyming from my monotony or is it my monstrosity, either way, everything suddenly honks as we are born pure in Manhattan, sometimes with the best of luck and I am not really sure where Hell's Kitchen is situated but it sounds marvelous, so I will go straight there, away from suicides trying to reduce the population explosion and this silent avenue.

Think of me as a downbeat, pictorially lavish, an urban hipster, a stylish clever swank, but with true grit, thus worryingly strange going to a tavern, some old ale house, where the owner once believed in the impossibility of men and women drinking together, so he nailed a sign on the door, No Back Room For Ladies, none, except for me inside this red brick tenement. Gas lamps illuminate my face, a bent nose and diving into a mug of ale warmed on the hob of the stove, with the barman, the most gloomy and stingy man in all of America, bragging about drinking only tap water and tea as he serves ale from the sagging bar, while outside the streets ail and flail and fail and pale into dingy rooming houses on Delancey for a smoke and a yawn and idle watching, look I do not give a damn, says the drunken short-order cook, slapping a burger on the burner which gives an angry sizzle.

These are titles of plays running together as one title.

Bumbug in the great god pan bare golden boy all that fall water by the spoonful and the songs I love so well Philip goes forth into grasses of a thousand colors by the way meet Vera cradle and all baby its you anything goes the normal heart sleep no more lucky guy tearing down the walls born bad the motherfucker with the hat after the blast burning doors the last match at office hour animal wisdom strange interlude the show-off too heavy for your pocket tiny beautiful things as you like it inanimate flea come from away measure for measure the terms of my surrender clever little lies fool for love spring awakening how to live on earth cloud nine hand to god desire amazing grace the new morality something rotten a midsummer's night's dream threesome John Ramona miss Julie whorl inside a loop informed consent dying for it between riverside and crazy I'm gonna pray for you so hard into the woods a month in the country the woodsman's honeymoon in Vegas on the town disgraced constellations a delicate balance the last ship it's only a play you can't take it with you wicked the river under the radar festival the elephant man a gentleman's guide to love and murder fish in the dark fashions for men placebo it shoulda been you long story short fun home remote in New York skylight on the twentieth century first star to the right made in China on the shore of the wide world one night only the terms of my surrender if only curvy widow the suitcase under my bed hello dolly a doll's house the play that goes wrong barbeque dames at sea drop dead perfect on your feet would you still love me if kill floor laugh it up stare it down pass the blutwurst bitte with Aaron's arms around me spiderman turn off the dark the break of noon black nativity now baby universe mistakes were made after the revolution bloody bloody Andrew Jackson metamorphosis angels in America time stands still ghosts in the cottonwoods women on the verge of a nervous breakdown scenes from an execution awake and sing Kafka on the shore a moon for the misbegotten once regrets hurt village beyond the horizon the big meal early plays death of a salesman Teresa's ecstasy blood knot Russian transport in summer shorts for Peter Pan on her 70th birthday before your very eyes dada woof papa hot Sylvia songbird reread another New York story.

Imagine me motoring to the Met in a 1947 Chrysler convertible. My life is of rich sauces, bubbly, hidden contradictions, a network of possibilities, shake my hand for I live in New York City, in boroughs of sentences, walking the talk, these nouns of a city of maroon nights, wearing New York's coat and scarf of deep blue leaping around me to hum blues in my ears, to whisper what are you doing here? Well, I am learning all the songs on that jukebox and buying cotton dresses at Anthology and plucking my eyebrows to improve myself, but not enough to attend an aerobic dance class that will rattle my bones, which is too much of every too muchness. Instead my heart beats in my chest at a cracking pace, I write poetry shuddering of awfulness about receiving permission to take my emotional support pig to The Ritz Carlton for cocktails, about muggy streets, searching for the Park Avenue liquor store that stocks a French liqueur from a vineyard where the winegrower attaches the wine bottle to a pear tree and the pear grows inside the wine bottle and after the pear is fully grown then the wine or whatever is added and we are left in wonderment as to how the pear came to be whole and adult inside the bottle and I first tried it at Daniele's place upstate and a man at her dinner party just hogged that liqueur and drank most of it which I thought was bloody rude.

I excel at riding the subway.

Every hour I spend in the fierce city is one less hour of my life in the sometimes quiet cerebral city I know so very little about, which I try not to think about, I think less and less, spending more and more time in the fall of bright orange leaves and the waning of ambition.

I never feel in the city that I am fading until a recorded voice interrupts the wait, train approaching the platform, my battery is low, in the red zone and I am not sure but that girl huddled in a dark corner might be shooting up, I cannot see her eyes most certainly ruined by love, my god the wheels are loud, why build a train with metal wheels, the train lurches, the old man asleep, his coffee spills in his lap and now a wet patch looks like he has peed his pants, the poor man, cheer up, this does not signify an apocalypse.

When I am not in love, I have bags of time to fashion intricate schemes, to conjure the power that rules the world, to find spaces of genuine whimsy, to cuss and refine a lifetime of neuroses, refuse an Instagram life, to think ah but the urban dweller loves the city and shaking up Manhattan cherry and whiskey, guessing blows downstream, guessing the amber of Jack Daniels, guessing no kitchens here if you're poor and a drop down bed are you kidding?

Right here, right now a mongrel blend refuses to believe God Almighty is a great shot, the exhausting high standards, be hearty, energetic with the appearance of a heavy drinker, be loud, optimistic in such an awful way, be fun and humble for this god listens to the new world's vinegary aspects of a city's tender feelings for matinees and comedy clubs and blondes wearing mink stoles, for the sophisticate eating the wrapper but not the candy. Here is the reality of excess, the waste, the free pours, the likely explanations, the apartment five flights up no elevator and women hitting the glass ceiling, the perfection of tulips along avenues, the spring in my step walking along Fifth Avenue and the commuters heading in the opposite direction.

And I climb out of a Chevrolet or limousine or that grotty Uber. Here the conundrum, the hyperbole, the dazzling phenomenon, the pain of infinite yearning, reality a vision liable to vanish, prepare to have your expectations exceeded with beautiful twitchy chest-swelling emotional impact, with reasons to be cheerful, with glib morbidity, with full-blown mania, sweat with pure grooviness and examine madness, a whack job in the light of reality. Tough love. Tough.

Here right now, I have accomplished the assignment of being a genuine urban dweller with a burst of interpretive dance and ritualized physicality and a motivated amount of eavesdropping.

stories

stories that grew from the notes

Remember another time? Another man. Let me tell you his name. My Scotty. Let's not talk about him. But we came here together here, Scotty and me, same as it ever was.

same as it ever was

A hit or two of bud. Pass the fuck out. Block it out. Cannot. Wipeout. So bottle the cockamamie. My romantic memory like perfumed smoke unfadable. Never gets as stale as songs and death. *Go on.* Uncork the genii moment. That wisp I relive over over *over* again.

Two tousling travelers, curly faces, tight jeans, black anoraks stoned some hungry wander of New York City. Romance hands entwine but sweaty inside cheap fingerless gloves. *Listen.* Shuffle hustle crowds, this busker taps bongo, cars brake, a cab driver yells, *indicate you asshole.*

I gaze into the yes! Truelove's bright buttony eyes. They must crinkle blue Mills & Boom. His intelligent nose, sandy hair, skinny body but muscles. Wasting. And me the plump hourglass girl, two dimples, green eyed, red lipsticked hey breathing in. *Mmmm.* Distinctive baking heavensmell airborne. Flare our dream nostrils. And pause. Toes wriggling footsore inside lairy socks sock it to me babe Bludstone boots. We knock-kneed outside a storefront of unassuming crumble shop tucked under a four-story apartment block on East Houston. Historied place. For one hundred years. Same as it. Ever. A grimy window pasted with faded newspaper articles yellowing edges. The owners much treasuring these many pictures of strangers shaking happy to be here, how do you do. Famous customers. Fabulous syrupy savory simple delectable. Like Us.

Then. Embroidery, filthy fur trimmed flows. And an unwashed urine-soaked long-haired freaky woman wafts past. Appears unbelievably blitzed sings creaky her voice,

Sign sign everywhere a sign.

I look up. See the sign. High. Above.

The Original Yonah Schimmel Knishery.

Original Since 1910.

OPEN.

Okay Shimmel or Schimmel easy. And writ. This slogan

One hundred years. Same as it ever was. Where a knish is still a knish. One world. One taste. One knish.

I announce with my flip flop flourish,

Here it is. The famous bakery where Leon Trotsky bought takeout yoghurt.

He strokes his beard of immense doubting.

Oh really. What flavor?

I don't *know.*

I imitate freak lady and twirl a sing at him,

You look like a fine upstanding young bloke. I think you'll doooo.

Adding a flat,

Ooh ooooh.

Song stops sudden. I see the good buzz. *I see* this artful display of goodies in the window of The Original Yonah Schimmel Knishery. Enormous tray of fresh knish things flaking music fluke, the crunchy jammy ooze beckons. Wow the vision mouth waters. Surfs the cheek pouches. Drools in public. My stomach rumbles under ratty shirt. Entire body salivates munchie growl. Ravenous wolfgirl. Of *desire.* Grab me seductive knishes serious to gobble. Greedy rubadubdub.

Let's get four. No six.

Man oh man, big chortle puzzling. Unable to define knish the why, the how.

So. What actually are these things?

My fine young man full of life then, thirty then, horny, then a bedsit ciggies giggle fucks of steamy hair-raising heights and howls and headies. Lie down, he says, And close your eyes. Three months left. Always that short time, stoner blaze laughing about minus entire knowledge what mysterious facts of knishes. And after loss what other lives force to live me missing. Him.

These things. Well I act the perky girl a particular unhelpful. My ill-informed.

I have no idea. Maybe some sort of handmade pie stuffed with you know.

No I don't.

Spices. Sweet. Zesty. Yummy. Stuff.

Him quizzical stares mystery unpronounceable.

Is the K silent?

I'm not sure.

From somewhere. He acquires another frown.

Well we are going to look pretty stupid saying 'knish,' if it's pronounced 'nish.'

Let's just say kernish or kanish.

He twitches self-conscious.

It doesn't sound right.

How about pretending we don't speak English?

Okay action zip and turn the lip key symbolizing top mute. Transform us plain speakers fast of a different language boosts our courage. We step furtive and enter The Knishery. A squeeze dowdy packed workers smells greasy breathy thickens hot air and buzzing crowd ignores us. Stupid tourists blushing in our duffles. I smile hopeful at a fat man leaning over the counter. He rubs bare hands on a grubby apron. Gets me fascinated. Those bushy eyebrows. Ruddy his face. Appley cheeks and cherub lips asking,

Waddya fancy lady?

Invisible cat-gets-my-tongue, Fancylady silently jabbing forefinger at the potato knishes. I hold up two fingers signal *peace.* I fake a guttural voice as if a Swede or Transylvanian or a foreign sophisticate pleading,

Pleeze.

Repeat the two-finger salute at the cherry cheese knishes. And husky requests,

Err doobledeaux.

Fatty hurls four knishes into paper bags and twists the corners gives impression of little piglet ears. We shuffle our dollars. Both retain speechless grins thank-you showing every sweet tooth.

Imposter foreigners happy hop outside. In the wintery streets. Our mouths tang buttery from the lightest filo crunch and salty strongest garlicky potato and luscious cherrycheese scrummy cherries stronger than me, a little sour divine mixes cream cheese sweetness

Be *strong* he says. I dare him,

Say it fast.

Cherrycheesecherrycheesecherrycheese.

I saturate delight trailing crumbs on the pavement. For him to follow. Love the city laughing fits there here and him hugs me biggest smooch hug.

Oh baby.

He will never. I wish. To breathe again. We of the shining hankering hearts well fed brainfuckingtastical magnificent deepest oceanlove. What I long for. Same As It Ever Was. The Day. Rare euphoria. Baked not ripped. Damn the comedown tenderly licks flakes from his numb fingers. Pastries live forever. Life sucks. I forget the awful tears. Remember. Fine young man. And kernish nish kanish knish tasty lip-smacking morning, willy nilly, hunger pangs, head change, random rambling the same as it ever is when. We Eat Our Words.

train of thought

An impossible journey toward love, I think is not in fact,
love. I think on a particular track, like a stink weed reaching
out to strangle choices or my apartment walls and wall lights
cut from crystal squeezing me beyond recognition as I step
into the night, hesitating, before choosing the path that
nobody chooses, picking at my wounds, running now to buy
ointment for my scabs. Don't look at them, ignore me and
what I think, that is what I think.
My eyes heavy with eyeshadow the colour of Kahlua and
cappuccino split hair, a won't-get-hurt girl discovers someone
begging for the lizard love on her laptop. Why not do him?
The online lover and however odd after meeting him fatter
in the city, his hullabaloo of disappointment at my shortness
shows in his creases. This man, a maggot wrangler, earns fifty
dollars an hour to breed grubs and place them on actors acting
as corpses in movies. You see, little maggots hatch on Sundays
and die on Fridays the same as shadows.
A film, a robot, the city of rationality remembers me giddy
as a goddess and maggot man dancing on stained carpet,
punching the jukebox as he upends packets of chips into my
open mouth of that Sunday, do I whisper,
Come home with me.
Why fling me on my lump bed burrow in the fresh linen and
rip shirt buttons baring an empty heart tattoo sitting on his
hairy chest, the probe begins, aware of his power, inquisitive
toes, grey wisps. His cry a desperate something, be my nurse,
vixen, doll. He blasts, spread your legs.
Darling drunk me has already and well-thumbed me, legless,
the trapdoor a soft body like a maggot not capable of running,
the rumpled sheets wet and damp concrete walls boast nude

art, the definition of hard nipples in my Target nightgown
needing more than one night and my place stinks to high hell
of cheap perfume the reason he holds his nose.
Where do you…oh…I can catch a train…maggoty bloke lives
upstate in Spring Valley Pearl River.

All at once, a quivering garden, the hush, somewhere in vases
on windowsills large peonies stare with enraged faces in Spring
Valley, I hear pearls really freeze. So wrap me in the cold river
rug, coughing more, winter, a red-knuckle beast.

I wear a cashmere coat, bobble scarf, crocheted fingerless
and hurry my killer boots hurricane into Hoboken Station.
Historic reflects in my mirror sunnies, thinking what great
mind decides, hey build the station as a freaking majestic
cavernous monolith. Look up, sings the skylight of stained-
glass accolades set in a wondrous cupola. Turn and turn
discovering copper sheets stamped on plaster walls. Go on
spin wonderful for a while, an hour early to absorb come
here, can someone, no one explains what classic, the elliptical
arches and touch motifs something misunderstood in the
ironwork, where cornice mouldings trace lost balconettes and
parapets.
At the ticket machine, I press the button harder and harder.
Fuck all this pressure to be good. Two tickets chinker out.
Christ. As if being alone isn't bad enough. Shall I ask the ticket
collector, stiff in his uniform, the frosting a militant black hat.
Hey Shiny, give me a refund, no? But I am in love with your
cap.
This crush rejection and the fact money disappears for idiotic
reasons. Expensive wine glasses dropped on the front step,
potted ferns left to die, designer jeans ripped at the crotch,

hundreds of dollars spent on opera tickets and we forgot to go.
And I think the reason to try dissolves.
Now the wait, with two tickets, I give one to a teenager of
indefinite gender who snatches it smiles with gratitude.
In the station waiting room, I find more more freak limestone
and bronze gentility, long mahogany benches scrolling a new
beginning. The delay, ice on the tracks. Kill me now, kill time,
kill twenty minutes in the Phoenix Bar and eat warm pretzels,
guzzle wine, wiggle to La Bamba, decline the Jägermeister
bombs of herbs, blooms, fruits and roots. Those buffalo
wings, scrawny chickens not pretty, nope, okay to hot whiskey
always must be scalding. Sorry. Bump into rushing passengers
grabbing quick popcorn, coffee, you want cream and sugar?
Spit lukewarm. Is everyone repulsive?
Getting colder and colder, I can't think clearly, allow madness
to warm me, yes that's me, full of shit bittersweet, wanting
more than anything to be inside my body, not this cage
of thoughts and I rush to search for reading matter for the
journey, doesn't matter, of course, it fucking matters.

Bye-bye sits in the window seat and peers through glass
blinded by filth and the train carries me uninvited to Spring
Valley, take me now train of solitary, the way a continuous
stream blinks bright lights flashing past and the bland freeze.
And the journey soon slows in the dark, my arrival at Pearling
River at Spring Valley whatever station for the train, the
spring, the pearls, the dreams are dead and all thoughts come
to a halt. I enter the nearest bar for what is shame.
And what if I find the worm boss's house and rap on his
knocker? Will the wrangler flick the switch and hide in his
closet? Or open the door, but keep the safety chain between
my shining embarrassment and his confusion asking, knocker?

Will the wrangler flick the switch and hide in his closet? Or open the door, but keep the safety chain between my shining embarrassment and his confusion asking,

Why are you here?
Will he leer at my breasts, knock my knees, extend his tongue through the gap in the door? Hear him bark, get wise, swallow painkillers, pave the way, skip the palaver. I think stupid, get back on the train, the wrong train and look I am moved by this particular track, knowing that rivers and valleys never slide past me. No kidding. It's the wrong stop, no pearls or springs, I think today is Friday. The miserable maggots. Is he waiting for me?
A wind passes like disappointment and goes away. Which way? I think with the effort of a breeze inside lightning. I think like a soap bubble aimless and transient in shock of where to go. Shall I pretend I am more than what I seem? Out here in the great silence with the hilarity of being tarnished.
Seems to be that river filling my eyes, wide with loss. The awful struggle to love as inseparable from the, oh right, the awful struggle. I think why again. I think give up again.
And hours later, it's the end of the line, the living end, nothing there, just me wondering, if I can't live without love, why aren't I dead?
Shhh. A ghost finger to my lips kissing shush in the shape of a tiny flower. Shhh. Think about the impossible as silly as reality. Just go back and make the best of thinking beautiful and alive and freezing and go to the city of a million possibilities. Tell this joke busting out of the shade, thinking so fucking what, for I have inside me this train of magnificent thought and all the brilliance of the world.

jelly legs

Lead me to water, to bridge that gap, to build my bridges, to Brooklyn Bridge marvel of the Industrial Revolution, its sweeping cables spanning the East River of wide over overly long. Brooklyn Bridge on Sunday is known as lover's lane. His longing to live the adventurous life. My desires more of tentative cafes and cake.

Hey, let's walk across. Everybody does.

A million people can't help themselves and surge forth. Stupid fears. My brain's sewn with fright sequins, picture that.

What, if it snows? Shame. And shouldn't we begin on the opposite side?

Our backs to the city doesn't make sense. Okay walk The Bridge same as anyone. Same as Jumbo the Elephant and twenty-one other confused elephants. Why in hell do elephants cross the damn bridge? Well to demonstrate strength and safety and the impossibility of collapse ends here.

He says, let's go.

Right. I reply from a tiny inner collapsing. Help. Get grip. Shake a bit, a twist, a big. My battleground. My Waterloo. Profuse trembles as plummet terror turns legs to jelly legs. He reaches for me, you'll be fine. Don't worry. Holds my hand. Clever man loves to touch me. Despite the symptoms. Sick to my curdling stomach. Paroxysmal positional vertigo oh this panic seizure of any heights. Not funny. Too skyscraping don't need thrills. Shrill thinking minor hysteria creeping drum roll *don't look down.*

So, I gaze the up. Winter sky, real sky, various cloudy real clouds very pretty lofty pale fluff above. Oooh see gothic those dark granite towers supporting a bridge too far, each end looms against, maybe force eyes to whoops unable to soar. These besting days he wants. Concentrate. Distract myself.

Scratch itchy bites. Burp. Crunch terrified gum like a cow on acid chewing cud. Fantasize about dying my hair mauve. Remember his hairlessness, his yellow kimono, the eruption of volcanoes. My body the earthquake. Our lack of secrets a good thing. Yes. Focus on the limp flags hanging from poles topped with brass baubles jutting from silhouettes of trusses. Somehow masses of steel suspension cables remind me of the black lace suspender belt, silk stockings, seams, costume swingtime party and us singing, groovy get down.

I put one footstep careful Christ! In front of the other like walking the plank. Stumble. This romantic stroll. Goosebumps goosesteps rigid along. Shambling my elevated battleground. Lovely arrrgh calling,

Wait for me.

He strides ahead. In his element.

Well the crossing takes a wobble forty-five minute agony. 1.3 nervous miles of pedestrian walkway. Where it. Seems forever. And the roar. Traffic fiend biggest trucks below on the second level. Parallels my mush legs. Freaking the way. Pink rims around eyes, tears from the blasting wind. Cold immobilizes *wait.* I can do this.

And finally, breathless vaporous. We reach the other side. Heaven this shudder. Bless shivers. Solid ground now. But the park is deserted and bleak.

It's deserted and bleak, I say, biting my lip.

Creates his disgruntle cranky.

Sorry.

I know, he sighs.

The empty landscape there calming. Snow like cotton balls clings to twigs. And dead reeds the color of hot English mustard poke through the ice.

Beautiful. I say. Coffee? Cake?
We search for a cafe. None. Pity.
He suggests,
How about we walk back over the bridge?
NO!
The view is better from here.
Screech mind.

Never again. He covers his ears and always a kiss. I reason. Think of the panting, the exhaustion and what is the point? To turn and go backwards with a stiff neck and a bubble of why do this torturous journey on my jelly legs.

But I see some understanding. Close by. There stands a solitary snowwoman. Armless. Naked. Overweight. Pregnant. Carrot nose poking out of the bright shine on her face. The weak sun reflecting saddest pebble eyes.

You're safe, soothes the snowwoman.

A stick plunging through her heart.

meditations of a solitary sweetheart

Joyriding through a crack in the hiccupping doom and somehow emerging in New York City. The perfect place to disappear. The city smells of a reason to live and I enter a kind of hyper-reality, a tangle of solitary meditations and a few visions, but those can't be helped, for I plan to think nothing but the analytical contemplation of thoughts that reflect the yapping of a mind stuck inside denial, like fungus growing on a lethal weapon, which sounds rotten and strange and not at all optimistic, so help me god, I will be all over the place.

I am staying on Eighteenth Street, Chelsea, in a vacation rental loft, pre-war industrial hip Pottery Barn airy space, huge windows, tiny crystal chandeliers, gilt-framed prints of birds and stains on the carpet of a new beginning, shivering on holiday, drinking wine, blinging out, taking the powder in an alcoholic cloud makes my body tick like a sleeping grenade and wondering why a shadow lurks behind the wallpaper stripes.

No fear. I have read The Yellow Wallpaper.

A man materializes, not quite the dreamy stud, his gelled hair spiking from under a beret. Is that a goatee I see? His cruel nose like a stallion on heat and he wears a black suit cut in the Frenchiest style, a tight fit, this blackness, blacking out. Of course, his name is Claude the Wanker, but I am not fussy. This two-dimensional paperman leans against the wall and rolls a joint. What a joker Pleasure is. Truth. And truth is sweet that's how it works.

Claude, tapping a cane, the air loaded with cannabis, Kafka and curtains.

C'est la vie mon amie.

It's curtains for you darlin'.

Sex brings out the worst in us. Claude taps his cane again.

Girls like to be spanked.

No. They. Don't.

At the sound of alarm bells, he backs off.

Sweetheart. Remember if you see strange visions tell no one. And whatever you do, don't walk into walls.

That's stupid. *Plonker.*

Men hate to be criticised. The wall softens, he gets tangled in the wallpaper stripes and flails about. Where are my scissors?

Claude walks through the wall. Shit. Forever this attraction to disappearing men. I grope after his apparition.

The Chekhovian first morning lies naked on the sofa, pressing knuckles to my breast and thinking. Why not be lonely or a loon? Why not go suck some bubbly downtown?

Thrill me going out with a burp, wearing a nylon windproof jacket over layers of frills and Doc Martins walking in the eye of the sidewalk storm. I am Whitman walking on the river streets of this courageous and friendly city of hurry. I walk fifteen blocks with an ache in my lungs and ice-cream at Morningside Park. Funny no-one here but an addict selling a stinking leather case to a gimpy man. I know that smell. Remember busting George the Greek? What a goofball, not enough moxie or too much, all too muchness eyes blasting like guns.

I see salt on the stoops of Brownstones and swagger me smokes a Salem, flicking the butt to the breadth and length of that bang metropolis.

Let me stretch my taffy arms to the tops of skyscrapers. Let my sugar flesh and candy bone zigzag through traffic choking Fifth Avenue. I will not go to migraine inducing Times Square of bump jostle screaming neon *Christ* don't go there, where a heart might tumble down one hundred stories.

Is there another word for up? In Lord & Taylor, a department store, the elevator man asks, Going up? To buy a baseball cap, a coat with a fur collar and ripped jeans. I sense a change in myself, I take a selfie, not so sweet.

Shall I create a distinct political vision, drink pumpkin latte, write an essay on grave-robbing, wear a bumblebee costume for Thanksgiving? Why a bumble bee? Because turkeys are still becoming extinct.

New York's deep blue coat and scarf leaps around me to hum blues in my ear, to whisper what are you doing here? Well, I'm learning all the songs on that jukebox and buying cotton dresses at Anthology and plucking my eyebrows to improve myself, but not enough to attend an aerobic dance class that will rattle my bones way too much.

Slam dunk a pimp with a manicure, ooh them cuticles lure a girl onto the rare tenderloin and find Fanny the lip hanging around the Metropole.

Here is the place radiating the glorious score of Swan Lake, to bake apple pie and baseball gloves, go see the Feelies onstage, make a splash as a lanky lying freethinker or moonlight as a cellist, banish all the anxiety over the cost of education, rant about broken elections. Here there is no such thing as a lady barber. Here I am alone and I wonder if I will be invited to blowouts, barbeques, shindigs, raves and meet-and-greets.

Hey dumb shit dumb ass, tell me your secret under the glow of a streetlight hanging low like a lost moon. I know now what it takes to discombobulate a city.

Let *me* give *you* directions. I will show you how to carouse your guileless at an off-Broadway opening night.
And yes stardom turns stars into assholes.

What about those billionaires, the bigwigs, the connivers, the cheats, the scammers refusing to reveal any the tricks of the trade?

Lipstick is the work of the devil, but not here, the painted women, fat shaming streaks wearing full length fur coats, red claws in place of fingernails and lashes wet from snowflakes.

There is a distinct fear of decrepitude.

Listening to buskers in Bryant Park, a Mexican trio strum guitars and the image of them makes me think of Picasso's painting, 'Three Musicians.'

And bathed in the false evening light, a hack from the seventies bellows Dylan's 'Murder Most Foul' outside Bed Bath N' Table.

Somehow I don't feel surrounded by water in Manhattan.
I ignore the lights across the bay, I do not walk to the docks, towards twilight and I am never followed in Chelsea.

Sometimes I hurry to the north south east west and soon I plan go near the edges of the city.

A beggar leaning against a trashcan on Union Square. His cardboard sign says, *Help I need money for weed.* I watch a woman give him a quarter and some fries. This is much better for him.

My nibble of the city tastes like pepperoni pizza, one slice for a dollar.

In Forty Second Street station, where an orchestra plays The Toreador Song so loud and urgent, commuters chomping on waffles keep time with the rhythms, feet not touching the ground, bottoms swaying through turnstiles, limbs twitching and leaping onto the E train, a metal monster screeching,

I'll make as much noise as I want!

God take me to the silence of Grant's tomb, but when I reach his tomb, the hush inside is broken by a punk blowing a colossal whistle, disturbing the emptiness and I hope that jerk swallows his tongue piercing. And his whistle.

I become tougher somehow, can you see me as a heavyweight with a brilliant soul and robust bladder.

Where shall I go to eat on my own? The eating-houses with tables for four, so I cannot sit alone with a bowl of thin soup, my solitude as thick as a piecrust in the indispensable noise and confusion.

What about Tavern On The Green? Oh no that place is too fancy schmancy.

I could try McSorley's, sawdust on the floor, the whine of an old phonograph with a charming face, a bent nose, where

I dive into a jug of dark ale, for the streets ail and flail and fail and pale into a dingy rooming house on Delancey, for a cigar and a yawn and idle watching. Look I don't give a damn, says the drunken short-order cook slapping a burger on the burner gives a sizzle. The barman smirking,

Lay off the booze, baby.

In an Irish pub midtown, Patty Brewster cries her thunder, eyes filling with stale beer tears, her lower lip trembles, she says,

I say stupid things. Men blame women for their desire.

Don't trip over the fire hydrants.

Always good advice. I worry she might go home and kill herself.

Minus two degrees rubs the colour from winter chutzpa as the dork of me watches the locals eat a Reuben on rye, buckwheat groats, kissing a saxophone in Dizzy's Club, munching a triple decker at Barney Greengrass. I linger on shy asphalt outside a diner stuffed with tousled Gap families brunching whoopee pancakes and crispy fat-free bitches on diets pretending to eat cottage cheese and sugarless Jell-O, apparently a favourite of Hitler's.

At Nathans, Coney Island yes I eat a whole hotdog and it's hideous.

The feeble man walking an Alsatian is yelling into his cell phone,

Morty Morty can ya hear me? We'll have to rethink the neck biting.

Her voice prickles my ear. Ugh breathy.

Excuse me honey.

Behind me, sandy streaks, peach lip gloss taupe pantsuit. Does her woollen pantyhose chafe the inner thighs?

Hi. I'm Betty from Wisconsin. Your scarf is trailing in that puddle.

I wince. Why can't I smile? And appreciate Betty's acknowledgment of my existence.

In a blaze of car fumes, a woman pushes a tired piano along Eighth Avenue. This straining creature will never reach her destination and how much I know *this*.

An old woman wearing a yellow shower cap, transforms her into a sunflower, except for a couple of gray strands. She stops to pat a miniature collie dog. The dog has navy and white sneakers on each paw. This dog and the woman, the sea and the sun, a picture of reconciliation.

Bubba Gump Shrimp, fresh seafood, family fun, servings the size of a boat. Who is Bubba? Silver bullets. A maimed body. And what is a Gump? Innocence. Stupidity. Lost in a forest.

Hiya.

Waiter Chad reveals rosy gums, his wart-free fingers smearing ketchup on a basket of fries.

Care for a smoothie, Ma'am? Run Forest Run? How about some Strawberry Shortcake?

In that moment my brain liquifies. And as I gobble popcorn shrimp, the filling in my molar falls out. A black hole remains. An infinite warped space where nothing returns. I read the promise printed on the tacky Bubba Gump menu. *We aim to please; if there's ever a problem we'll fix it.*

Can you fix this hole in my universe?

A Manhattan, cherry and whiskey, I'm guessing blown downstream. I'm guessing the amber of Jack Daniels. I'm guessing no kitchens here if you're poor and a drop-down bed, are you kidding me?

These vinegary aspects of New York City a mongrel blend of exhausting high standards, be hearty, energetic, with the appearance of a heavy drinker, be loud, optimistic, fun and humble in an awful way. Grow tender feelings for matinees, comedy clubs and blondes wearing mink stoles, eating the wrapper but not the candy.

Here is the reality of excess, the waste, the free pours, the likely explanations, the apartment five flights up, no elevator and women hitting the glass ceiling.

Here the conundrum, the hyperbole, the dazzling phenomenon, the pain of infinite yearning, reality a vision liable to vanish, prepare to have your expectations exceeded with beautiful twitchy chest-swelling emotional impact, with reasons to be cheerful, with glib morbidity, with full-blown mania, tough love, sweat with pure groovy lunacy, a whack job in the light of reality.

Here fire engines wail as if they have lost their first born child.

The apartment windows are without curtains, everything can be seen, murderers hastily washing meat cleavers in kitchen sinks and stuffing bodies into bin bags. The wife always cops it.

In the shadow of a fifth-floor walk-up, a chain-smoking figure presses his face to the window pane. The tip of his cigarette smouldering red. We face each other at twilight. Two lone voyeurs. Me eating a Twinkie and him slouching on the razor's edge.

Oh Jesus.

In MoMA, I ride the escalators hurry, hurry to modernity, where uncertainty bites the brightness of Ensor's tormented painting, The Intrigue and cooks and skeletons fight over a scrap of herring. How savoury.

A figure appears. Hello Herman. The man sports a navy jacket, bowtie and long grey hair. Perky. Cadaverous. Hippy.

Are you a faggot or a poet?

Herman carries a human head on a platter and from out of its mouth pokes a fish tail garnished with lemon slices. The head makes me think of moussaka and it's all too much. I am on a diet. Herman asks me,

What are you trying to be?

Intriguing. And less lonely.

Herman goes back to his red herring. The man standing next to me shakes his head and walks away from this madness.

On the bright side, the MoMA café serves almond meringues. And the cashier doesn't let on that they automatically add the tip, so most people like me end up tipping twice.

An intriguing girl nods perceptively at Willem De Kooning's, Woman 1 all violence or passion, which is not the usual genteel painting of the female form. Some see the painting as a degrading or powerful depiction. Christ she's creepy. Is this how men see women? Scary with crazed eyes, grinning fangs and an underwire bra supporting breasts like garbage sacks and multiple arms, so useful. I love her. Woman 1 crashes though my mind, enters my soul, its hot as hell in there. She smothers me in a riot of brush strokes, keeping the colors the same pinks, turquoises and gullible greens. Woman 1 transforms Sweetheart into the absurd abstract of splatters, scrapings, fury and spontaneity. And weak at the knees. Is this de Kooning's sexual frustration or mine? That day in MOMA, following the exit signs, searching for a way out.

Sweetheart jumps into a taxi and arrives in a flurry of De Kooning colors at The Chelsea Hotel, colony of Bohemia, avant-garde poets and rive gauche writers.

In the lobby, an ashen-faced boy hands me a smile on a dish of desire. Not Leonard singing to Janis, *I remember you well in the Chelsea Hotel.* Instead, with eyes like pools of mud, he sings,

I've been dreaming of you, sprinkled with sugar.

Queen of the mist, a Venus in fur, Sweetheart is not prepared for a mud bath.

The concierge at the front desk leers, go home sweetheart.

Creep.

Two starry dynamos, Sweetheart and Woman 1, tiptoe the corridors of the hotel, past the rooms of Nancy's stabbing and Dylan's fatal whiskey. Warrior Woman 1 slaps the sad-eyed lady of the lowlands and commands,

Don't sweat it, honey.

My room in the Hotel Chelsea has a grimy linoleum floor and lemon-colored walls. I hang my coat with the fur collar in the wardrobe of hope and dump my suitcase on the bed. There are enormous lumps inside the mattress. A sugar-lump sees my reflection in the mirror of Absolute Reality, angel-headed hipster Woman 1, wanting the ghosts of the Chelsea to saturate my stranding and all the time I act as if I have never had a serious thought in my life.

These meditations bounce off the city's fierce light. Happiness can strike anywhere. In this dream, New York understands the wild in my eyes and Woman 1 burning in my soul.

A solitary city with the persona of a Grand Duke, its high-rise complexion, dead straight streets, wide blocks, hair the color of smoke and smiling a golden sunset asking,

Have I kept you waiting?

Here's to thinking things through, to radiant delusions, to living a solitary life and chasing after myself, falling, flying, flipping inside my own gravitational force. Goodbye to candy, paper stripes, leaping tigers, and the fear of never meeting the right person as a solution to loneliness. I love a city. This illusion of my date with New York, I am wearing a midnight dress and a scarlet petticoat, my hair coiled in a demure knot, not sure if my legs are mine and clinking glasses in the Algonquin Hotel, major bucks for a glass of champagne, far too slick for a gussied sweetheart beating time with a bread stick to all that jazz.

the same as everything dying is an art

The time comes when my ex-husband's money I love to burn, runs low, but I am still a bit rich, a fraudster artist dunking pretzels in gin, my rude elbows on the bar in The Dog and Duck, local pub with a sticky counter, Formica tables and sick lighting from a stained glass window of a spaniel barking and a duck quacking cheers drinking from schooners of beer creating an ambiance of mockery. Behind the bar, the barman pops up and down as if dodging bullets in a firing line. Pow Pow. And across the street the handy art college insinuating itself into an historic jail might be a challenge.

Why? asks the barman twirling the most horrible moustache.

What are you, a magician? Anyway, the question makes me wonder, why in the hell not. Because the reality of myself, being an artist, fancies a new life or two, hindered at present by my imagining it could be true that according to ancient Taoist's it is important to preserve a man's semen and return it to the brain, that suckerfish attach themselves to ocean liners and slow them down. An artists thwarted by the fear of impending tsunamis, pandemics, this withering mess of a planet too far gone, the possibility of a Chinese invasion. Who is there to protect us? And my fear of love, of being swept away in the arms of a myth, a strong gardener, some Neolithic man, then falling hard, lapsing into nothingness, freaking out about a future melting me down, transforming my body into a different animal, a good woman who single handedly holds up the world, forgives herself and hates people who say, emotional roller-coaster.

The barman strokes his hairy lip.

Why?

What?

Blink blink this is realty possessing a hairy lip asking for a reason and already I've had enough of this nosy fairy so I take aim.

Shut up.

Dread keeps me company walking home, visualizing the amount of sky it will take to crush me. The clouds crumple onto the roof of my divorce apartment groaning with the weight of pointlessness.

Is a letterbox really necessary these days? Or the bespoke kitchen wallpaper of medieval blues, an antique chopping block, two Japanese prints and a bronze galloping horse weathervane spinning on the balcony for Christ sake.

All this crap surrounding me, the boho woman wrapping myself in silk scarves, loads of bracelets and a kimono concealing a plump body, the opposite of delightful, lying in bed, 600 thread-count sheets, linen duvet and smoking weed giving me a complex lusciousness, red eyes and thin hair, discontent combing my split ends and thinking what a tangle. What an excellent merlot. What a view of the city at night.

Hullo my new friend, the art of foreboding boiling within me. Which means an imminent meltdown for the dangle marionette, a nuisance to my own self, a mess, messing on purpose, beyond caring, spitting out gum, farting and inhaling wine until my body blazes and the stain of a moon does nothing to help me change into a fearless woman.

And don't get me started on life flashing by at the speed of whatever. The disbelief, rejection, eventual success and at the end, forgetting to leave a note. All the while looking in all the wrong graveyards for an insatiable love that is instrumental in causing me to wig out, go bonkers, both and moaning the almost poetic, how I've had enough of dudes jiggling blood-pumped stiffies.

Well, so god help me, what is the shape of my hunger? Okay, a man to tweak my earlobes and muss my hair with such gentleness that it is almost painful. A man that doesn't fiddle with himself. A guy who plants snowdrops and lilies in the moonlight. A human being who doesn't leave a week's worth of underpants on the floor. Is that too much to ask for? Is there such man on this earth?

More and more, the reality is that a misfit woman befriends beautiful women, mouthy girlfriends, such as Regina, wine cellar, folded napkin, I mean business type; Stella, bleached pubes, topless on the beach; Madison, organic soap in the shape of a rose, all her chakras aligned for no particular reason. Unsympathetic. Oblivious. Cumquat airheads. Cocksure and freshly shaved slappers. Their mwa mwa air kissing, draining me of soul.

Poor Fliss. Alone again. This weekend? No. We have plans with our partners. You'd be the odd one out.

These suckerfish friends fastening lips onto my failures, urging,

Go right on ahead Fliss. Drown your sorrows.

At least they provide the plonk, the perfume, the lazing about and the bullshit lies. The universe loves you. We are in this together. Don't be a chicken. The chicken soup is boiling over. Are you mad?

Loneliness prolongs my hollow scream. The har-de-har booze refuses to freeze, and the wise whiskey goddess advises me as an artist, to draw a picture of a sharp axe and give those girls the chop.

Bye bye hangers-on.

The artist freak of me must create *something significant* over the course of a lifetime like recreate the blotches of a brain and it's billion neurons, paint numbness in the form of a boat disappearing into a lake of tears or paint bruised apples, bloodied wounds, a dagger a la Caravaggio representing overreaction, spite, envy and regret skulking in the shadows of a shroud covering a dead man in the bath. My goodness. Too dark. Cheer up. Go for it. The Happy What. Paint light glimmering through a canopy of trees, dew drops, possibly daffodils blooming under sunshine, a cat licking her paws in anticipation of eventual passion and happiness.

I present this portfolio of artworks to a panel of professors lording it up at The National Art School, a college of some repute, remember the one across the road from the Dog and Duck. The interview consists of four disinterested men staring at me and fingering my appalling efforts. And I somehow get accepted. Don't be impressed. I'm not that special. The college admits anyone owning a credit card.

Welcome to The National Art School, heritage buildings, the jail cells hiding behind The Gates of Hell where centuries before, prisoners came in with foolish grins, condemned to three years hard, carving crosses, fish shapes and initials into stone blocks under a brilliant sun shining down on public hangings, the corpses swinging from nooses in the breeze of relief.

Now one hundred years later, curved sandstone walls keep the art students insane, working below roof beams like the spokes of a wheel shot through with the marks of malice, chalk dust rising from paint spattered floors, easels abandoned at awkward angles. Where moth-eaten taxidermy of rabbits and foxes sit on studio shelves alongside plaster busts of Greek goddesses with perfect tits.

In the first week, I decide to make friends, so I approach a sculptor, her face like a stopped clock.

Hey Irene, what did you do before art school?

I killed my girlfriend.

Oh my god.

I didn't mean too.

The younger students splash paint onto their khaki overalls and scamper about like circus performers. Others pose as bohemians sipping cappuccinos and smoking clove cigarettes and worshipping the devil. Enlightenment and pretense is plentiful. And lonely women such as Mona quoting Henry Lawson, poet and former inmate.

The prisoners came in with foolish grins. Hear hear to the pig drunk poets.

Mona turning thirty-two, born gifted, hoping it's not too late to be discovered. Mona with pencils poking out of her top knot. Her cherry blossom face, slim waist and predatory green eyes always on the nearest bottle of wine. Her paintings of figs, storms, empty beds translate as abstract masterpieces of deft composition and rich tones. I interrupt her scribbling on her sketch pad as if she's about to be poisoned.

Hello. I'm Fliss Hyde. As in Jekyll and Hyde, only nicer.

Hi. Mona. Rhymes with loner.

Is that a hint?

What are you drawing?

Broken toys.

Wow. That's original.

She looks up at me and I begin bleeding words.

Before I became an artist I was a failed art historian. I'm divorced. Twice. The first one had an enormous, you know, appetite. And the second guy was a cockroach. I've lived in Cyprus, London and Boston. God knows why I came back to Sydney. I'm planning to move to New York. See that bloke over there? The janitor. Watch out for him. Pervert. Anyway, I park the exe's Merc right outside the Gates of Hell and feed the meter, then rush out at lunchtime with a rag soaked in turpentine and wipe the chalk marks off the tire so I won't get a parking ticket. How's that for ingenuity? Fancy getting a coffee? And I should tell you most of my family are dead. Which helps.

She licks her lips revealing tiny teeth.

Mine too.

There are many things a woman should not know about another woman. Yet our differences keep us inseparable. Mona lives in a rundown apartment with dirty white walls, fragile teacups, the rooms sparse of furniture, outside harsh street lamps illuminate filth on the windowsill. Mona organizes hundreds of letters, lists, receipts and notes into neat piles that shriek obsessive. She exists on sickness benefits, her anorexia, depression and hypochondria paying the rent. She never marries, doesn't have a boyfriend or a driver's license. Mona dresses in the kind of black that kills color. On pleasant days she accessorizes with a white silk scarf. An image of elegant gothic about to surrender. I notice her bitten fingernails and hands raw from excessive washing. I wonder if she keeps a weapon in her handbag patterned with zebra stripes.

What's in the bag?

Mona reveals an airtight container filled with almonds, raisins and dates. She confesses,

I get hungry.

I sigh.

Don't we all.

In the ceramics class, a Chinese boy with the air of a terracotta warrior, shapes clay to resemble a perfect human ear. Twelve classes. Twelve delicate ears. At the end of each class, he crushes the ear with his mallet.

A metaphor for self-destruction, says Mona. No-one listens to him.

I reply, No one can understand him. His English is terrible.

The students meet at a derelict warehouse on a wharf beside the harbor. We sketch lapping saltwater, a boardwalk, pigeon poop and weathered walls.

Jesus, I mutter.

Crouching in muck and glass shards under a broken window, my fingers black from charcoal savagely drawing an industrial lampshade. Trot it out, bang it out, beast artist bellowing. Get the light right.

Mona lies in the sun telling everyone and no one,

I am not inspired.

And she falls asleep.

On Wednesdays, the life drawing class makes my nose run, makes me sneeze from this allergy to nudity. Adonis the model, his buttery skin and caramel curls mesmerizing the homosexuals and older female students. Adonis recites Dante's The Divine Comedy, the more a thing is perfect, the more it feels pleasure and pain.

Bollocks, I say and Mona laughs.

I'm confused.

Great, I say. Confusion is brutal. It disrupts the brain.

Adonis falls asleep, his gentle snores keep time with Mona blurring the outlines of her perfect drawing.

Envy consumes me. I tell myself, to feel envy is human. Draw him quick. Conte for depth. Graphite for shade. Murder the figure. Smear titanium pastel over the muscles, skin, knees, magnificent smudges ghosting the man. The teacher circles shouting,

Perspective! Proportions! Concentrate on the fine art of balance. It's a male. Erase those breasts.

I fall of my chair. Split the seams of my skirt and crash into a moment of shame, disturbing the focus of every student. Mona frowns.

What in hell are you doing Fliss?

I flinch from her anger.

Adonis now awake, strokes his balls and offers a helping hand. His dick level with my averted eyes. He heaves me to my feet. I say,

Oh my God, it's this tragic skirt.

He whispers,

Take it off.

And he thrusts his hips, clicks his fingers and transforms his body into a ripple of water.

After class, Adonis confides,

I've bequeathed my skeleton to the college.

Which leaves me speechless, yet wanting to ask, are you dying.

When the painting professor instructs the students to paint a self-portrait, I want to set him on fire. I think, please not that.

It's too invasive. I'd rather paint a picture of Neptune eating a snickers bar. I'd prefer to paint my own guts.

I choose a canvas fifty inches square, this won't take long, it's all about the immediacy so begin faster with a shaky contour, cropping the jaw and layering paint to expose the cheek bones of a cave-woman, slosh seawater eyes, add the glow of jaundiced whites. Whoa missing eyelids, paint them in the softest plum. Let the left eye bulge from its socket. A pretentious eye to flatter my vanity. An attempt to convey a concept of seeing the beyond. Dilute the remaining colors letting them flow down the canvas. This melting head dripping fluids, my jealousy leaking from within at the sight of Mona's self-portrait. What life has done to her. How she sees herself. The tortured brilliant artist. A face bomb about to explode. Swollen cheeks, trip-lines for veins and grey tears depicting the weeping of a self-whipping martyr.

On the stroke of twelve, Mona paints a black hole where her heart should be. *Bam.*

The teacher announces,

Lunch break.

At the thought of food, Mona begins to sob.

Mona's portrait eats her alive. Her laughter disappears. She cries for what she does not have, lovers, babies, money, silverware, success. The woman coming apart. Why in the name of God, in that state of mind, does she douse herself in Plath? An outcast on a cold star enclosed in a wall of glass, unable to feel anything but an awful helpless numbness.

Days later, the beautiful leper hardens into the beautiful grenade. The reality, every ambitious woman wants a fleshy, forgettable friend. I catch her staring at me.

The happy hour at The Dog and Duck, far from happy, where the art world hobnobs with students. The random slap and tickle. Black ale threatening nausea. A jukebox fifty cents a song. *I still wish you ooh ooh ooh the best. Fuck you.*

Be brave, I tell myself, go and chat to Nigel, an important curator. A gaunt bloke wearing the art world uniform, blue jeans, grey T-shirt, tailored jacket and Italian loafers. The hint of eyeliner, does me in. Why do I find him so intimidating?

Mona dolls it up at the bar. She spies me with Nigel. She grows inquisitive horns, stamps her little hooves, froths past tables and charges miss kaboom across the room. The jukebox plays *s'wonderful s'marvelous shaboom boom.*

Ooh he's a spunk. She grabs my arm,

Hey Flissee sweetie. Introduce me to your new friend. Helloooo.

She elbows me.

Ow.

She pushes me out of the way.

Darling, get us another drink. I'll have a double vodka no ice.

Mona and Nigel indulge in slick repartee. She giggles, her nipples beading through a flimsy blouse. She lights up a Camel, blows smoke and mirrors.

Oh you know who? I'd love to meet him.

I stand there, the glass woman, still intact but shattered. The world becomes static, detaching me from her. Invisible Fliss caught in the twilight of an empty field. The art animal running across my heart roaring treachery. I crawl across the ugly carpet to the restroom and puke up my rattlesnake jealousy. I allow Mona to steal my chances. A fraud does not raise hell. She avoids confrontation. A psycho artist seethes and festers. Does this make me a fuck up? Yep. Pretty much. And so fucking sad.

Nigel picks up the check and they disappear into the night.

Forget reality. An art coward writes a note, a sludge of hate to a toxic girl smelling of linseed oil. A note for crying out loud. Pages of tight-fisted resentment. A spiteful paper knife through her delicate emotions. *Dear Mona self-absorbed narcissist deceitful nothing more to do with so completely a cunt friendship la la la never speak again.* This overblown rancor. The shock of me acting in haste. I should have understood. I should have known. Selfishness is her art.

Regret cries for dead friendship. Mona the cold star. Imagine her in a moon suit and funeral veil. Imagine her writing back to me. Her tearful voice, *what's the matter? What have I done?*

One of the students tells me she burnt my letter and flushed the ashes down the toilet. Ashes to dust to futile. The crowd of her watching blackened fragments swirling into the sewer of my meanness and bloody-mindedness.

A year later, the fast year, a drowning-in-wine year, the piss-art year, the night wears a silk dress patterned with violets and polka dots, a hint of cleavage, leather ankle boots crack a whip and I therefore head out to a fancy party. Picture a crowd of tuxedo fuckers, vermouth conversations with slices of orange, reeking of conceit, the hoity toity socialites and surgical procedures in abundance, plus a barman, waiters, waitresses, caterers, microscopic food, loads of alcohol. That sort of raving shindig.

A waitress brings over a tray of cocktails. The mirror ball spins tiny lights across her face. I recognize the lines of sadness at the corners of her lips, her perfection, her thinness. A diminished soul, no more than a bare branch. The white streak of defeat through her hair. She has done this to herself. Those quivering hands. The rattle of martinis not quite crashing, not quite spilling. My guilt pleading,

Listen. I need to explain…

Something closes inside Mona's eyes. I never knew you. She pretends to smile.

You look nice.

I am not nice. I am Hyde and Jekyll. I am a two faced bitch. I want to beg, we can still be friends. But for her silence. She unsees me as if from a desolate ocean, as she is a remote cloud. I don't blame her. Her slow and deliberate turning away, avoiding me and disappearing without closure, this penance and my callous decision, there is nothing now but to drink and get laid.

After many cocktails, tripping clumsy Holy Fuck, dropping my martini, smashing the glass into broken stars and ruining the suede shoes belonging to a man resting in a deck chair.

Shit I am so sorry.

The moon shines on a tanned face, steel hair, brown eyes with noble flecks twitching at my heart and my eyelashes bat a lusty gawk. He grins and offers his hand.

I'm Vincent.

Of the starry starry night. My throaty response,

Fliss Hyde.

Can I trust his finger on a trigger? What if I cry? What if he changes the song? Am I careless? Tossing my heart of glass to a stranger. Do not ask these questions. Flicking my hair like a bimbo. Luring him into my slapdash unravelling. Vincent leans closer and takes my hand.

Careful where you tread.

Vincent, down-to-earth man of the land, a landscape gardener, a hint of rain on soil, secret gardens, parsley, sage, rosemary, thyme. He confides,

I made a mint.

Good for you, I say, confused about the mint. Oh right. Money. He means money.

The midnight bells ring party time intoxicating the air, the two of us taking refuge in the empty basement. Overhead the razzle-dazzle jazzing our explorations. More wet arching. Vincent. And a thirst for plants this desire writing inside my blood. My insides race and collapse, an ache unfurls the warmth, the kissing of eyebrows, the impression of heatstroke across my body. Yes we are bonking. Yes I am crying. Yes I'm dramatic, howling from within for his touch ends a long isolation and in the end, I think, not bad.

Let's dance, says Vincent. *I'll Be Around.* Upstairs, *when you're falling down and can't find your feet* the slow dance begins. The sound of a harmonica ricochets through the room. Hey switch on the smoke machine. Clouds and knees mingle. This flurry, the whispers. Vincent, I swear wears the wings of an angel. He says,

You're awesome.

He says,

Let's run away together. It will be fun.

It's not a question. I bat away the swarm of doubting. I fall down on the dance floor and tremble a reply,

Okay. Let's go somewhere gorgeous and faraway, but with television.

Time travels to a place sifting the winter sun, raging sirens, church bells *fine so fine* New York, this skyscraper city cools inside my head and I look down at the park pinned under snow as sunrise shifts from faded pear to bright orange, bombarding the shadowy spaces rubbing my eyes. Vincent starry starry calling,

Fliss come back to bed.

A lovely life now. I close my eyes. My magic carpet skims the leafless treetops. A splendid ride of steady gentleness, sleeping late, easy time, nothing doing. Honey glows. Butter melts on fruit toast. I am marmalade. I am almonds soaking in milk. I am a blown kiss. I am sugar dissolving in Manhattan.

In zero temperatures, cold enough to stop a squirrel's heart, we walk along Central Park West beside creamy buildings, proud giantesses, snow banks heaping against curbs. Commuters in padded coats hurry on slippery surfaces. An old woman walks a poodle, its violet galoshes like burning little beacons. We surprise a snowman, stick nose, startled pebble eyes, heroic demeanor, not a thought in its frozen no brainer.

Wet traffic sounds soothing. Rain soaked streets reflect the red green red green of traffic lights. Taxis, school buses, raincoats dance abstract yellows in this city more vibrant than a triple scotch.

Our traction boots skid up the grand steps, pass the pillars, into the majesty of the Museum Of Natural History. We see an exhibition about the human brain, displaying neurons with the power to reignite unhappy memories. I make my fingers into the shape of a pistol pointing at my head, bang bang, the phantom of remorse.

On this day, I learn that inside the hippocampus, neural systems control thoughts and intellect exists in the moment and the human brain weighs as much as a rock melon. Vincent pats my head.

A billion neurons race through your rock melon at two hundred and fifty miles an hour.

Yeah I feel them.

We pause before the Hominids scraping blood from animal skins. Are they more human than ape or more ape than human? Furry women, inside a cavern, behind a glass wall. Are they friends? Does a million-year friendship last? Should complicated women form intense attachments?

Vincent sings on 72nd Street, famous for slaughter. *Just a perfect day, drink sangria in the park, when it gets dark, we go home.* My cell phone beeps, an unknown number, *hello Fliss, I thought you'd like to know what I am planning to do this morning.* The voice fades. The time difference is sixteen hours. Her plan, it is already done.

The shock of Mona's last words sinks into mud and slush outside the Dakota building. And I am staring at a sort of light. Why do gas lamps burn such pretentious flames? A doorman stands motionless in the darkened vestibule. His gold trimmed cap glints. I stand where Lennon fell. *Imagine all the people.* His last words, *yes I am.* What would Mona say with a gun to her head? Just you wait.

Vincent smokes and waits on the corner. Stamping his feet to keep warm, he mouths,

What's wrong?

He leads me across the road to Strawberry Fields. Forever, a teardrop zone, *let her take me down*, remembrance, the unbreakable circle and that single word, Imagine. Her message, *I thought you should know.* Mona this is not a game. I have so much guilt. My neurons slow. Not so fast abundant brain, heavy as a melon.

That night, the years drain into my pillow. I dream of footprints in the sand. Her wild laugh, the ravaged self. Stones in her pockets. *No note. No explanation. A single cry rising like a balloon.*

Early morning in the park, the sorrow of storms overnight transforms the trees into icy skeletons. A man and his Rottweiler leave deep foot and paw prints like a string of inkblots in the snow. I step into each one and drag my feet, gashing the snow. She lost hope. Vincent keeping his distance and calling,

Why are you so upset? Why do you care so much?

And I am shouting,

I always believed I could make things right with her.

The past, present and future blends into a billion neurons. I don't want to think of Mona amongst the ruins, her fraught mind falling apart. Forget the cold star at her easel. I crawl from the hole in her painted chest. Why not churn past the grief towards some invisible peace? Maybe now is the time. The golden days of drunken rain, of someone missed here in New York, where wind from the north carries snowflakes creating the coldest winter of the century. The winter of why. The winter of what I remember. What I invent and then springtime brings entrapment, a global pandemic sneaking up on us, an unwanted shock to awaken the human race, this virus closing the world forever, locking us inside, forcing the quiet, the contemplation, the facts, life is lovely and then it is not.

So I become a body beginning to melt. I think, melting moments are supposed to be delicious. But melting hurts.

Change throbs with pain. That sting of adjusting. Imagine the phantom of myself thawing in a universe, never the same. Because scientists' claim, melting is equal to the space, separating atomic layers in a crystal. They say surface atoms lose stability. They say regret heats internal energy turning it into liquid like my eyes, nose, body oozing tears, blood, mucous, bile. I am the molten state transforming into the rounding globe. Into the disturbing spectacle of an uncertain future flinging me past the limitations of my own life. Imagine, the same as everything, dying is an art. And the solid earth incomparable saying, forgive yourself. Forgive me.

In reality, I close the front door. We stay inside the apartment and wait. Remember? You take me into your arms, into your arms, into your arms.

Oh Lord, for a brief moment it is enough.

For Maureen Duffy, a friendship lost.

The Yack Yack

Acknowledgements

These acknowledgements ascend from my entire being to the sound of trumpets, ringing bells and clashing cymbals, as transcending all the love, kindness and generosity on the planet, giving me the inspiration to leave something behind for the two littlest darlingist Miss K and Moo, I promise to be with you forever. And heart for heart and soul the soul for giving me hope, more hope, the luxury of hope for just being yourself thank you, New York City. Dear Desmond W. Ferguson thank you for being by my side. This magnificent two, Chris and Helga Holland thank you for the time spent in your wonderful apartment and for cheering me on. The deepest unfathomable cavernous appreciation to Nikki McWatters and Karyn Maslyn for your incalculable help. I bow down to all the amazing literary journals and their editors for their dedication and support of literary fiction and who published my short fiction. Thank you to editor Emma Warnock for including my story Twinkle in the No Alibis Press 2019 anthology, Still Worlds Turning. Thank you to my New York family, Viviane, Gerald, Daniele, Nikos, Debra, Stefan, Su, Ram, Marcia for all the great nights, great food, great wine for your greater than greatness, it was a pleasure and a delight to hang out with you in New York. And all my love to Ben Sewell and Sally Moreshead for your guidance, patience, for being so sensible, for being wonderful parents to Katherine Rose and Maximilian and the same amount of love to the fabulous Grant Collins, quirky Sasha and whimsical Hannah for being yourselves and helping me to understand the process of retail. (don't ask)

This book owes its existence to the exceptional Stevan V. Nikolic, Editor Adelaide Books. My deep thanks for his encour- agement and for publishing *The Yack Yack.*

Also by Judyth Emanuel

"A multi-layered journey through place and soul"
Nikki McWatters

"Saturated with smart and brave prose"
Marcia Butler

About the Author

Judyth Emanuel is the author of two novels. Her short fiction has appeared in many notable literary journals and several anthologies. She is currently completing a collection of poetry. www.judythemanuel.com

Made in the USA
Middletown, DE
20 February 2023